The (New) American Way

The (New) American Way

MARK R. ADAMS

Columbus, Ohio

The (New) American Way

ISBN (paperback): 9781642377507
eISBN: 9781642377514

Contents

This book is dedicated to all the servicemen who gave their life for this great country and to all the military branches that protect us every day.

ର   ର   ର

I would like to thank my wife Shari for tirelessly helping me prepare my book for publication and for the 38 years of marital bliss.

Chapter 1

THE BEGINNING

A large crowd lined up outside a suburban neighborhood bookstore. Most of the people standing in line held hardcover copies of a book entitled *The (New) American Way*. Upon the glass window at the front of the store was a poster showing a large black and white photo of an early middle-aged man wearing a sports jacket and a button-up shirt. Beneath the man were big bold letters spelling my name: Adam Marsh.

Sitting at a table in a bookstore in Charlottesville, Virginia, (at age 45), I glanced at stacks of *The (New) American Way* on either side of me. One after another a multitude of patrons approached me for an autograph. A nice-looking 30-something woman steps up for her turn as I ask, "And what is your name?"

"Diane," she answered. I nodded and began writing a short note inside her book, and as I finished, she continued, "I truly think you are a hero, Mr. Marsh. All my relatives agree and we've got liberals, conservatives, and moderates."

I almost blushed while answering, "Oh, that's very kind of you to say."

Diane added, "What would be terrific is if the ideas in your book could actually come true."

I smiled a little bit, which revealed a buried sadness within my gaze and answered, "I'm right there with you on that one." I gently slapped her book shut and handed it back to her.

Smiling, she moved on allowing the next patron to step forward.

It was a teenage boy. "Who are you?" he inquired.

"I'm Adam Marsh, and this is my first book *The (New) American Way*," I proclaimed. "It has topped the best-seller list for 14 months now, and I'm, to be honest, quite humbled by its success. I mean, I'm not the best writer in the world, but I do have a passion for my ideas," I concluded.

Another teenage boy joined his friend, and he said, "Hi, Mr. Marsh."

"You can call me Adam," I told him. "What's your name?"

"Teddy," he said, "and this is my friend, Eric. Is there a movie coming out, based on your book?"

With a puzzled look, I answered. "We just signed the contracts last week. Between you and me, I think that's why this line is so long."

I winked at the boys and Eric said, "Nah, man. I think it's because people want things to change."

I nodded and thought, Wow, what a smart kid.

As the boys left, a man in a black suit stepped up to the table. He placed his copy of my book down in front of me.

"Who shall I make it out to?" I asked.

But strangely the man just walked away. My eyebrows lowered as I watched the man leave. I was bewildered to say the least. I looked down at the book and opened the front cover to find a note written crisp and dark that said, "Meet me behind the store after the signing." I tried to mask my concern and placed the book aside. I put on a big smile for the next customer and continued to give autographs for the next two hours.

As I finished with the last patron, the owner of the bookstore came over and said, "This has been a tremendous success. I really appreciate your professionalism and patience with my customers."

I told him, "You're welcome, and thank you for the opportunity to sell a few more books. By the way, do you have a back door here?"

He showed me the back door, and I told my driver/bodyguard to meet me there with the car. I waited a couple of minutes for the car to pull around, and then emerged through the exit. The man in the black suit was smoking a cigarette and checked the time on his phone while leaning against his black SUV.

My driver joined me just as the guy said, "I didn't realize you'd be bringing company."

"My wife tells me I should hire security," I said.

He proclaims, "There's nothing for you to fear, Mr. Marsh."

He stepped toward me, only to be met by my security guard, who asked, "Is there a problem here?" The man glares at my guard then reaches into his jacket pocket and pulls out a badge.

"FBI," he said.

My security guard said, "How do we know that's real?"

The agent snapped the badge shut and bragged, "I'd be happy to prove it. I can have 50 of my fellow agents here in 10 minutes." The guard looked at me and I told him to take it easy and let me talk to the guy alone.

"I'll be okay," I said.

"You sure?" he asked

"Yeah. Give me a few minutes," I said.

I turned to the agent and asked, "What's this all about?"

He answered, "My is name is Craig Archer and I'm a great fan of your work, Mr. Marsh. My colleagues, too."

As he shook my hand, I replied, "Wow. Thanks. What a comforting thing to say."

Craig inquired, "Can we have an hour of your time?"

"Who's we?" I asked.

Craig stared at me and reassured me, "We are your friends, Mr. Marsh. All of us are your friends. We want to give you a chance to do something great for our country. From reading your book, we get the idea that you are a take-charge kind of person that gets things done. We have a proposition for you, but it's not my place to present this opportunity. I'm asking you to please come with me and meet with the people who sent me. I will take you back to your hotel as soon as the meeting concludes. You won't need your driver any more tonight."

Getting in a vehicle with a strange man goes against everything I had been taught. I don't usually put myself in situations in which I don't have control. Without my driver and security, I was taking a big chance, but one thing convinced me to go with him: He never checked me for a weapon, and I was carrying my 9mm pistol. I had a conceal-carry license and seldom went anywhere without a gun. Traveling around a country that is so polarized, one can run into a lot of people who disagree with almost all my ideas. I figured if Craig wasn't an FBI agent and meant to do me harm, he would have checked me for a weapon.

I decided to go with him. I told my driver," Go to the hotel and wait for me. I'll check in with you every hour. If I don't, call the police and tell them what happened here."

He nodded and wished me good luck. I got into the black SUV with Craig feeling a bit uneasy and on high alert.

We drove for about 45 minutes toward Washington, DC, and finally pulled into a parking lot of what looked like a government building of some kind. There wasn't a single car in the parking lot. If I was meeting a group of Craig's friends there, they must have parachuted in. He walked me into the building with a flashlight. He turned the lights on as we walked down a long hallway. We entered a room with a long conference table and Craig pulled out a chair at its head. He turned to me and said, "Sit here," and headed toward the door. "I hope we get a chance to meet again. Maybe next time I'll even grab an autograph," he said as he winked and left the room.

So many scenarios were going through my head as I sat in that room alone; the walls naked, no logos, pictures, or symbols. Where in the world was I? After a couple of moments that seemed like forever, a stream of military officials poured through the room's door. Army, Navy, Air Force, Marines, Coast Guard, Reserves--you name it—they were all there. Even the CIA, NSA and FBI had representatives there. What on earth did they want with me?

The last man shut the door behind him and made a point to lock it; once the chairs filled up, men stood lining the blank walls.

Across from me sat General Scott St. Claire. I recognized him from appearances on TV from time to time. He addressed me, "It's a pleasure to see you here, Mr. Marsh."

My mouth was so dry I could barely answer, "I hope I can say the same."

The men all laugh. The General proclaimed, "Oh, yes. You don't trust the government much, now do you?"

I replied, "I certainly haven't made that a secret."

"Well, we have," said the General.

Looking a little puzzled, I asked, "What do you mean?"

"It's simple, said the General. "We don't trust the government either, but no one knows that except us," as he points around the room. The room was silent for a moment. I nodded my head as if I were starting to understand where they were coming from, but I was still confused as to what they wanted from me. The General continued, "It worked for a long time, more or less. But what we didn't realize for all those decades was that the government's functioning depended, to a certain extent, upon the honor system. People agreed--consciously or otherwise--to look out for the public's interests when they got into elected office. Nowadays, however, it's party before people and ideology before common sense."

"You sound like you've been reading my book," I replied. The room bursts into laughter and I was beginning to feel more comfortable in my surroundings.

"We've all read your book, and I've read some chapters more than once," said the General.

"Okay, but what's that got to do with me being here?" I asked.

The General answered, "We've had something in the works, Mr. Marsh. It's highly confidential and has been going on for just over a decade now. We intend to overthrow the federal government."

I couldn't believe what I was hearing, but I had been saying it for years. Since America was more than 20 trillion in debt and politicians lining their own pockets with no regard for the hard-working people in this country, I *knew* something like this was possible. I had predicted that if something like this ever happened, it would be the military that carried it out. But why me? I looked at the General and said, "You're kidding me, right?"

And with a most stern look on his face, the General replied, "No, Mr. Marsh. We are dead serious!"

"How do I know you guys are even who you say you are? I mean, I got driven here by an FBI agent, maybe, and put in a bare room to sit down with not one recognizable person. How do I know this isn't some kind of set-up?" I asked.

The General replied, "In time we're hopeful we'll gain your trust. If you like, I can orchestrate a ride in one of our new tanks, but for now let me say this . . ." The General stood up and walked around the room and turned to me and said, "We have the military capacity to overthrow the government. We could put our plan into action within 72 hours. It's been rehearsed, perfected and we have buy-in from leadership at all levels of command. However, what we've lacked for all these years is a public face. We need someone popular, someone the people trust. According to the data we've compiled, you're tracking as the most trusted American since George Washington. Elvis ranks a little bit higher than you, but hey, you can't mess with the king."

I closed my eyes for a few seconds, as I understood what my part in all this would be if I bought in.

"We need a leader," said the General.

I replied, "You mean a pawn."

"Excuse me, Mr. Marsh?" said the General.

"Look," I said. "I have a lot of political concepts, but I've never lead more than 15 people at one time in my construction business or kids on the basketball teams I coached. You really think I'm leader material for an entire nation?"

The General responded, "You've turned your construction business over to a foreman. You could give it away considering the residuals you've received from your book. I feel you have lead more like 40 million people considering the book's popularity."

"I'm here just because so many people like my book?" I countered.

"Like your book?" the General asked in astonishment. "This isn't about liking some novel. If that were the case, we'd have brought Stephen King in here. You wrote a book about a new direction for this country. With some minor quibbles, it happens to be the precise direction my colleagues you see here and I have been pursuing for quite some time: A government of the people, for the people, and by the people. The real deal, though, not just symbols and fairy dust."

"What am I supposed to be, king?" I inquired.

"Don't go competing with Elvis now," said the General. Everyone laughed except me. The General returned to his seat and said, "You'll be the commander-in-chief."

"The President?" I asked.

"No, technically, no. On a formal basis, we can grant you commander status and you can run the country however you like. But only the people can elect a President. We trust you will run the country with a common-sense approach like the fictional characters in your novel. So, you can issue executive orders under martial law and run things your way."

The Air Force commander spoke up, "For now." There were chuckles in the room, but General St. Claire was not amused. "That's right, for now, until we get things straightened out, and then we can start over," said the General.

"So you are saying I can change laws, strike down laws, get rid of regulations as I see fit, and run the day to day operations of our federal government. I will have to deal with foreign policy, domestic issues, and answer to you guys?" I said.

"No, you are the commander-in-chief. We take orders from you. We trust your judgment. You will be the face of the takeover. You give us an order; we carry it out. We believe you will be successful," the General declares.

"You know this is treason and we could all be arrested," I proclaimed.

At that point everyone was laughing and the Air Force commander said, "Who will do the arresting. Everyone with that authority at the federal level is here. This is a "fool-proof" plan. We just want you to front this."

"General St. Claire spoke up, "Just think it over, you don't have to answer now."

I replied, "Okay. And suppose I say no? Will I disappear, I mean, after all: I could go to the police and tell them about what happened here."

General St. Claire smirked and said, "Yeah, but with all due respect, who would believe you? You're a storyteller, Mr. Marsh, a man of make-believe. Unless you decide to make this real."

I stood up and told the entire group that I appreciated their confidence in me and that I would talk it over with my wife and make a decision soon. General St. Claire gave me a phone number to call if I needed to talk with him anymore or to give him my final decision. I called my driver and told him I was on the way back with Agent Archer and not to worry.

I had a lot to think about.

My wife had already called me ten times. I'm sure she was worried, but I couldn't explain it all on the phone. I texted her and told her the book signing ran over and I couldn't talk. I told her I was tired and going to bed, and would see her tomorrow when I got home. It was going to be a long conversation and I dreaded it. My mind was going 100 mph about the pros and cons of the offer. I had to think of my family, but what about my country? It could be the chance of a lifetime, to make a difference for millions of people.

I doubted that I would sleep that night.

Chapter 2

HOW I GOT HERE

How I got to this point in my life is an amazing story, yet that wasn't the half of it. Writing a novel was the farthest thing from my mind when I was in college. I just wanted a degree and a job teaching school, so I could coach basketball and golf. That all came to pass, and I experienced some success. But as time went by, I learned some valuable lessons. The most important of these lessons was that there wasn't much money in teaching and coaching. I was sort of known for not playing well with others. In other words, I needed to be my own boss. So, I turned to the only other thing I knew much about: the construction business.

After a couple of years of renting an apartment, I decided to build a house to live in. I was teaching and coaching in my hometown in Alabama, so I was familiar with the housing market there and knew it would be a good investment. I hired a contractor and watched as he coordinated all the different subcontractors to erect the structure and finish the inside. I thought to myself, this is something I could do if I ever wanted to quit teaching. I could hire a crew and subcontractors as good as my builder. To make a long story short, after two more years of teaching, I started my own construction business and left the education field for good.

In the early stages of my construction business, I was building spec houses. I had my own house up for sale, and I was putting up another one to move into if need be. I was lucky that I knew the bankers in town and they were eager to loan me money to get started. And timing was everything in construction. Just as I finished the new home, the house I was living in sold. I made a tidy profit and moved into the newly completed home. But another important life lesson was learned as I parted with 6% of the sale price to the real estate agent. Taxes had to be paid on my profit. Having employees was a new experience and not a particularly pleasant one. Taxes also had to be paid on their payroll, along with unemployment insurance. Worker's Compensation Insurance was extremely high for the construction field. Was there going to be any left for me? And worst of all, every problem my employees had, also became my problem. If Employee Smith's wife had a hangnail, he would have to take her to the doctor since they only had one vehicle or she couldn't drive. Business liability insurance was expensive, and construction permits, inspections, and fire and theft insurance were all mandatory. Being my own boss had its benefits, but also its own set of problems - and it didn't seem that the government wanted to help. Health insurance for my employees was out of the question under the Affordable Care Act, a.k.a. Obamacare. I could have probably attracted better workers if I could have offered it, but the cost was prohibitive.

While building my tenth house, I stopped long enough one-day to visit my CPA to check on my tax return. As I walked to the back of the office building, I passed one room that gave me pause. Sitting behind a new desk was the most recent hire at the CPA firm. Her name was Cindy Hawkins. I had known her in high school, but she was just a freshman during my senior year. I stopped and asked, "Are you Cindy Hawkins?"

She replied, "Yes, and you are Adam Marsh."

I couldn't believe she knew my name, but believe me, I was thrilled. She was gorgeous with her long dark hair and tan complexion. At 5'8" and 120 lbs. she was perfect. I'm 6'5" and 230 lbs. of sexy. I had to get her story from Dan Wilkins, my CPA.

'It's good to see you, and I would love to hear more about how you ended up here," I proclaimed.

"Maybe Dan will let me work on your return and we can put you on the clock while we catch up," she said as she gave me a wink.

"I'm sure Dan would love that!" I chided. "I'll make an appointment." I waved over my shoulder as I walked back to Dan's office.

As I took my seat in Dan's office, Dan said, "I didn't think you were going to get past Cindy's office."

I answered, "I won't next time. What's her story?"

"Cindy is single and has recently broken up with her boyfriend, and if I wasn't married, you wouldn't have a chance."

I laughed and said, "You might be underestimating my sexual prowess." Taxes were the farthest thing from my mind, but we did manage to finish my return. But that was the luckiest day of my life because one year later, Cindy Hawkins became Mrs. Adam Marsh. Of course, I built her a new house, and we started our life together in our hometown. I owned my own business, and she understood the money side of that business. We were a good pairing with unlimited potential.

My background included two amazing parents. I was raised by a hard-working father and a perfectionist mother. Both were very demanding with regards to my grades and sports. Church was also a big part of my upbringing. I attended services regularly until college, then like many young people, my church going lagged. My parents expected me to apply myself to the best of my ability and never give up. I was taught to adapt and persevere and this showed in my construction projects. I expected employees to work diligently and smart, and I struggled with those who didn't have the same work ethic. Quite often Cindy had to endure a rant on the deficiencies of several of my employees or a sub-contractor. I began to blame our government for part of this problem. People were receiving so many subsidies that they had no incentive to work. Employees were hard to find and subcontractors failed me several times due to their inability to hire and keep good employees. All this was starting to change my way of thinking about our government. We needed to reverse course on several of the paths chosen by our leaders. But nothing was getting done to solve any of our problems due to gridlock at every level of government. Something needed to change, and it did – Cindy got pregnant.

Having children was an awesome experience from the first day I found out my wife was pregnant to the actual birth. There is no doubt that a change came over me when I became a parent. I realized that someone besides my wife was counting on me providing for them and keeping them safe. I began to think long term. I wanted them to be my legacy when I was gone. I wondered what kind of world they would grow up in and someday raise children of their own. Cindy delivered a son who we named Drew and two and a half years later came Natalie, our daughter. I was under the gun now more than ever. Cindy still worked, but I needed to build more houses to provide for my growing family. I was perfectly willing to work as many hours as needed, but the housing market could change overnight. A hurricane in Florida could raise the cost of building materials all over the country. The Federal Reserve could raise interest rates, which would all but stop borrowing for building houses.

All this was making me increasingly nervous about the direction of our nation. Would Social Security be around when I retired? How much longer could I afford health insurance under Obamacare? It seemed as if I was paying a premium for four or five families so that the government could give away subsidies to deadbeats that wouldn't even look for a job. Something had to change, but what could I do? I had no interest in politics. I couldn't run for office. I could think about what I could do, but life gets in the way. I had a wife and two children to take care of, and I couldn't just up and quit on them.

So, I came up with an idea: I would write a novel about the overthrow of the government. It would be fiction, but within the story would be a blueprint that, if followed, would fix most of the problems we were experiencing in our nation. There were problems caused by Presidents from both political parties. There were problems caused by Congress and activist judges wanting to exert their power over the President. And none of them could ever come up with a solution because all suffered from a lack of common sense and reasoning.

Also, there was another huge problem with this plan: I am not a writer. English was not my strong suit in school, but with spell check and Cindy's help, I might just pull this off. Another problem was finding the time to commit to writing the story on paper. I didn't ever learn to type, so I had to print every word on a legal pad. And as usual, when I focus my attention on something, I get the job done. I stayed up late and woke up early to put my story on paper. It only took me about 2 months to get the basic ideas down, but the finished product ended up being a 6-month project. I had built houses in less time!

The process of finding a publisher was not an easy one. Coaxing someone to read a manuscript was difficult. I contacted several publishers that had no interest in reading a book by a novice such as me. But I persisted and finally talked to an editor at Gilles Publishing named Marshall Lanerie, which gave me the break I needed. He loved the book and recommended it be published ASAP.

My book would provide answers to some of our country's difficult issues. They could follow my direction and the country would get back on the right track. My children would be able to prosper in the greatest country in the world. I'm sure the solutions in my novel would be considered extreme, but in my opinion, extreme measures were needed to fix the problems at this point in time.

Chapter 3

MEANWHILE, BACK AT THE RANCH

After the meeting, I returned to my hotel. But with unfamiliar surroundings, aggravating traffic noises, and visions of a black SUV with FBI personnel watching my door, I was correct – I couldn't sleep.

I left Charlottesville in the middle of the night and drove home to Alabama. I arrived at lunchtime and the kids were still at school. It was mid-November, so tax season was still a couple of months away. I called Cindy at work and told her to come home.

I said, "Dan won't mind. Tell him I missed you so much and I couldn't wait any longer to see you."

Cindy laughed and proclaimed, "Hey, I'm a partner, you know, I have some clout around here. But why do I need to come home immediately? Is there something wrong?"

"No," I answered swiftly, "but it's an opportunity that must be addressed by tonight and we need some time to discuss it. It's a little complicated."

"Okay," she said, "I'm on my way."

That was the best I could do so as not to alarm her. Ten minutes later we were face-to-face. She was more beautiful than the day we married. At 42 years old and with a 16-year-old boy and a 13-year-old girl to worry about, she went to work every day. She had been a perfect wife for me. I didn't want to mess all that up, but here goes.

Cindy hugged me and gave me a kiss. I went back for seconds and she looked at me and asked, "What have you done?" and laughed.

"Nothing," I replied, "or at least nothing bad. I have to tell you what happened to me last night after the book signing. Sit down and let me get started. This may take a while."

Cindy sat on the couch while I walked about the room explaining the whole scenario. I could tell she was shocked as I laid out all the details.

"Are you sure they weren't a theater troupe?" she asked.

I grinned and answered, "I thought of that, too, but the one General, General Scott St. Claire, gave me his card. I looked him up online and he has an office in the Pentagon."

Cindy blurted, "Oh my God!"

"Oh He wasn't at the meeting, at least in person, but I hope He's watching this," I replied.

Cindy said, "You can't do this, Adam. It will change our lives entirely. The kids will be at risk!"

I answered, "I know. I've thought about that. But what about the country? It's falling apart. The Press hounds the President day and night. Congress won't help him. The judicial system puts up roadblocks at every turn. This could create a better place for our children and their children's children."

Cindy argued, "its one thing to write a book and get a movie made, but to make your fiction into reality . . . I just don't know."

"Look, sweetheart," I replied, "you knew this novel contained a blueprint to right several wrongs in our government. Someone finally noticed who could actually do something about it. I think this is just the natural progression of our style of government. You need to stop and adjust it every so often and the time is now."

"But you are talking about overthrowing the U. S. government. You could be killed, Adam!" Cindy argued.

I answered, "I know this sounds crazy, but if I'm killed while making the world a better place for our children, might it actually be worth it?"

Cindy started to cry and she walked over to hug me.

"Let's sleep on it and talk a little more in the morning. The kids will be home soon," I said.

It was a long sleepless night.

The next morning it was all we could do to act as if nothing was wrong and get the kids off to school. Drew, our oldest at 16, had a Ford pickup and could drop off Natalie at middle school on the way to his high school. Drew is an amazing kid. He is a starter on the varsity basketball team at 6'4"tall and plays guard. Natalie starts on the high school girls' golf team while only in the 8th grade. Both are straight A students and leaders in their classes. And while I admit to being totally biased, both are extremely nice-looking like their mother. They were typical teenagers—very busy, very popular, and always in need of the newest technology. However, we didn't just hand out money; we made them work at their sports in exchange for an allowance. As long as they practiced each day and applied themselves, they got most of what they asked for. The trade-off in that arrangement was the college scholarship awaiting them. If the plan worked, neither they nor I would have to pay for their college educations or diplomas.

As soon as they got out of the door for school, Cindy and I checked in at our jobs, her CPA firm and my foreman, and we sat down to discuss the situation at hand.

Cindy looked at me with those beautiful eyes and said, "Well, I didn't sleep much last night, and I know you didn't either. I really don't want to disrupt our family, but I know you feel strongly about the direction our country is going, and if anyone can fix this mess, it's you. I can't make the decision for you, but I will love you no matter what you decide. The children will adjust because they are smart. Tell me what you're thinking. Convince me we are doing the right thing."

On September 11, 2001, the world changed for everyone. I was 27 years old with a new wife, my own business, and life was exciting. We both wanted children, but wondered if we could be good parents in the world we were living in. We were optimistic and full of hope, but then the towers fell. As a history teacher in high school, I understood how this could happen, but our country had not been attacked on our soil since the Mexican War from 1846-48—a war fought over property: the annexation of the Independent Republic of Texas. This vile act of knocking down the World Trade Center towers was a terrorist attack based on a radical religious philosophy. The radical wing of the Muslim religion of Islam coordinated an attack on the towers and the Pentagon.

In my opinion, this was the last time the country experienced bi-partisanship. It was nearly unanimous voting on a joint resolution in Congress to give President George W. Bush the authority to do whatever it took to hunt down the people responsible for this heinous act. A couple of years later, Congress voted to go to war in Iraq to keep Saddam Hussein from using weapons of mass destruction and spreading terrorism throughout the Middle East and the rest of the world. The weapons were never found and the bi-partisanship soon faded. These events changed my attitude on politicians and politics forever.

Cindy waited for me to speak. We had discussed politics now and then throughout our marriage, but I needed to go in depth on how I felt about things today. It was critical to this decision that she understood where I was coming from. I wouldn't ruin our marriage and family. She must be on board or I just couldn't do it. I loved her and the children too much to alienate them. "Sweetheart," I said, "I need to tell you a long story; some of it you've heard before, but let me finish before you speak. After I'm done, we will decide together."

She nodded in agreement.

I began, "After the hotly contested election of 2000 and the *"hanging chads"* debacle in Florida, the Democrats felt they had been cheated out of a victory. George W. Bush became the 43rd President of the U.S. Nine months later the terrorists attacked the twin towers. Bush's popularity soared as he took measures to keep us all safe. Everyone wanted justice served to Al-Qaeda, the terrorist group responsible for the attack. Its leader Osama Bin-Laden was the most hated and hunted man in the world. The military chased him in Afghanistan and almost captured him, only to have him slip into Pakistan and into hiding for many years. Then came the weapons of mass destruction report from the CIA. They accused Saddam Hussein of developing or attempting to purchase nuclear weapons. Eventually Congress voted for going into Iraq to defeat Saddam and find these weapons of mass destruction. I looked at this entire situation and applied common sense. If the CIA lied about the weapons of mass destruction, it had to be for a reason. But what exactly was that reason? Did Bush 43 just want to finish what Bush 41 started when Iraq invaded Kuwait? Saddam should have been overthrown then. Maybe we really did believe Saddam had WMDs. If it were so important to prove the CIA correct in their lie, wouldn't they have planted some WMDs that we could "find?" That was all very strange; our attention needed to be on Al Qaeda and Bin Laden. But they didn't come out and fight as much as they hid themselves in remote training camps. The longer that went on, the more the media began to accuse Bush 43 of using the false CIA reports on WMDs to go to war in Iraq. Then Hurricane Katrina hit New Orleans. Everyone was warned to evacuate; however, many did not. Bush didn't respond to the crisis soon enough to suit the Democrats or the media. During his last two years in office, Democrats controlled the Congress. He signed their legislation into law and in his last year of office in 2008, the mortgage crisis hit our nation. It caused a banking crisis and threw us into a recession. Relaxed banking regulations through Democrat legislation pushed banks to lend to people with less than stellar credit scores. The banks were not without fault, but that should have never happened. The Dems blamed the entire mess on Bush. That paved the way for the election of maybe the most unqualified person to ever be elected President, Barrack Hussein Obama. Hope and change was his election motto. He was going to have the most transparent administration ever. Now you know I have never been a racist, so my dislike of that President was based on performance, not the color of his skin. The media adored this man. He came out of nowhere. Where were his college records? Was he born in the US? Was he even a citizen? I gave him the benefit of the doubt for a while, but things were happening that didn't add up. He didn't unite us; he divided us. The liberal mainstream media turned a blind eye to every scandal and misstep he made. None were worse than the lies he told to get the *Affordable Care Act* passed, right before the Republicans took power back in Congress. The signature legislation, which he wanted to insure his legacy, was health care for everyone. Nicknamed Obamacare, which pissed-off the liberal Democrats, the law was based on several lies. The key architect of Obamacare was Jonathan Gruber. He admitted that it was passed by exploiting political ignorance. President Obama knew he was lying when he told the nation, "You can keep your policy, you can keep your doctor, and we will save a family of four $2500 per year." You know I can't stand liars and thieves; President Obama qualified as both during that ruse. Here he was, running up our deficit to $20 trillion, increasing it more than all other Presidents combined, and lying right to our faces. That was the straw that broke the camel's back for me. I started to pay more attention to why the Republicans were obstructing this liar-in-chief at every turn. The polarization of the electorate had created the widest divide since the Civil War. The media was only fanning the flames and I wanted to do something about it. I wasn't going to commit treason or call for an overthrow of the government. But I decided to write my novel to at least issue a warning of what could be coming if we didn't start solving problems in a bi-partisan manner. I couldn't believe Obama was able to win a second term. Was the Republican Party so out of touch with the people that they could never win a Presidential election again? I was never so glad to see 2016 roll around to see if the Republicans could save the U.S. from the leftists that had taken over the Democratic Party. Hilary Clinton beat out a self-proclaimed socialist, Bernie Sanders, for the Democrat nomination, but not without some underhanded tricks in their debates. She was secretly given the questions prior to one debate. She was a terrible candidate with way too much baggage. Benghazi, email servers, Uranium One, and the mishandling of her husband's affairs, just to name a few. Remember, I predicted her defeat by Trump after the Republican convention. But now look at our country; the media hates President Trump more than it ever hated George W. Bush, and I didn't think that was possible. Now the Democrats are obstructing, saying turnabout is fair play. The biggest battlegrounds are selecting Supreme Court justices and border security. Could things be much worse? I think the military sees a chance to fix this nation and they need me to help them. Can I really turn them down? It's not just my sacrifice, I know. It will be everyone in our family. It will be our parents and grandparents, our children, and especially you and me. So tell me what you think."

I had rambled for quite a while and Cindy just listened. She knew how conflicted I was. She also knew that if I decided to get involved, I would see it through to the end to the best of my ability. I added one more thing, "Honey, I think I can do this in one year and then let the country and the people start over. After that, we can go back to our normal lives. I think I want to try it."

She came over to me, had me sit down, and got in my lap. She smiled and said, "I have always admired you for your strength, your truthfulness, and your convictions. When we married in the church and I said for better or for worse, I meant it. I have never loved you more than I love you at this moment. God will watch over us; I really believe that. Do what your heart tells you; I will support your decision to the fullest."

I kissed Cindy like the first time we went out and told her to make preparations to move. I would give her the details when I found out what was next. "Just go to work and try not to think about it, and I will call you in a little while," I said.

Chapter 4

THE DECISION IS MADE

A s I sat at my desk in my office at home, I tried to imagine what it would be like to lead this nation. I needed to make sure I would be allowed to make decisions without question. I couldn't procrastinate any longer. I had to call General St. Claire and give him my decision. I took out his card and called the number for his office.

"General St. Claire's office; how may I help you?" answered his aid.

"Good morning. General St. Claire asked me to call him today. My name is Adam Marsh,"

"I will have to switch you. Hold please," he said.

At the gun range, the General fired a semi-automatic rifle toward a paper target, shredding it to pieces.

As he finished he took out his ear plugs and shouted," I love trying out the new weapons each year."

A military aid approached him yelling, "Phone call for you, General; an Adam Marsh."

"You don't have to yell, private; I've taken my ear plugs out," he laughed and said. The General handed the rifle to the private and headed to the nearest building. He entered an office with a telephone on the desk, which is blinking a red light. He took a seat, took a big breath, and picked up the receiver.

"General St. Claire here."

I was sitting at my desk alone and responded, "This is Adam Marsh; I guess you remember me." I couldn't help but laugh at that statement, and the General was amused, too.

"Yes, I remember us having quite a conversation," he answered.

"Is this a good time for us to talk a bit more?"

"This line is totally secure, with a zero chance of anyone listening without permission. You can speak freely, and thanks for asking first. This just proves to me that we've chosen the right person for this job. You think before you speak! So, how are you this morning?"

I answered, "Kind of low on sleep, if you know what I mean."

"I do," answered General St. Claire. "And I understand. You probably discussed the matter with your family."

"Well, my wife, yes, but kids have a hard time with secrets," I said.

And then the General asked the big question, "Have you come to any conclusion?"

I took a deep breath and asked, "General, can you assure me of 100% full security?"

He replied, "Number one, my 'team,' is the entire U.S. military. And number two, you'd get twice the protection of any President in our history. And of course, this extends to any family members that need protection."

I told him, "Sir, my mother and father will need it, along with my brother and his family."

The General interrupted me and chuckled, "Adam, you will be in charge of this nation's entire military apparatus. If you want your parents in a steel bunker a mile beneath the ground in Utah, we will make it so."

There is a slight pause, as the General anticipated my answer, and I took another deep breath. "General St. Claire, I'm going to do this."

General St. Claire sounded very pleased and said, "Thank you, Commander Marsh."

"Whoa, whoa, whoa," I said. "Hold up. Don't call me that just yet. Isn't there some kind of swearing in ceremony?"

"This is a revolt," replied the General. "We're a little less formal than that."

"How can I be sure you won't rise up against me?" I asked.

The General exhaled and answered, "Fix this country, re-train its citizens, and just follow the blueprint you laid out in your book. It's why we chose you in the first place. Don't let power corrupt you. Work for the American people and you will get nothing but loyalty from your men, myself very much included. Follow the plan; we've already read your book. We know some of the things will seem radical at first, but we back you 100%."

"Okay. So, you promise to take all my orders, hear all my ideas," I said.

General St. Claire replied, "I will give input or feedback if I think you're misguided as will others who share my rank, for that is my job as a patriot in service of a democracy. But rest assured, you are and shall be our authentic commander."

I proclaim, "In that case, I will see you tomorrow at your office in the Pentagon. Tell them to be expecting me. I'll come alone. Get people here to set up security around my family prior to the takeover."

"Of course," he replied.

"Let's say 1:00 p.m.," I said.

"Yes, sir," answered the General. "And if I may say so, I'm proud to be an American once again."

"I'll see you soon," I said as I hung up the phone.

I had to pack and get on the road. Cindy would want to be there, but I couldn't chance it. Something could go wrong and I didn't want her there. The kids were still in school, and I knew this was going to disrupt their normal routine in a big way. Cindy would have to handle the home front until things calmed down. She would have to get used to security being around 24/7.

I drove to Dan's office to pick up Cindy for an early lunch. I went into her office and shut the door. I whispered, "I told him I would do it. I have to be in Washington, D.C. tomorrow by 1:00 p.m. You will have to stay here with the kids and explain the situation to them. I will call you tonight and fill you in. Just bear with me until things settle down. The kids need you and they have lives to lead here. Nothing I'm going to do should affect Drew's season, except for the extra security around him. He can handle it, as well as Natalie, with your help."

"I want to be there with you, but I know you're right," said Cindy.

"Kiss me goodbye; I've got to go. Please watch yourself and the kids, and I'll call you tonight. Don't tell the kids anything until it happens. Just tell them I had to go out of town for a book signing again."

"Okay. I love you," said Cindy.

We kissed and hugged one last time, and I left for the capitol.

Chapter 5

OFF TO THE SWAMP

The anticipation built as I reached General St. Claire's office at the Pentagon. I never thought in my wildest dreams something like this could happen. I showed my driver's license at the front desk, and I was escorted to the General's office. He greeted me with a smile and the door closed behind me.

"How will this go down and when?" I asked.

The General answered, in a firm tone, "At 0900 hours Monday morning the military will move into every city in the country. Every branch will have a part in the takeover. Washington, D.C., will be the focus."

"That means I have two more full days to prepare myself for the avalanche of reporters what will befall me sometime Monday," I replied.

"You will have the full attention of the nation because every network will televise your first address to the people. They will be hanging on your every word. They are going to find it strange that a non-military citizen will be in charge, but it's really the same as the President being Commander-in-Chief. We are just changing leadership without an election for the first time," replied the General.

We talked for a while longer and the General had his driver take me to a hotel. He dropped me off, and I checked in with a pre-arranged reservation. The desk clerk handed me a key for my room. As I got about half way there, I turned and went back to the desk.

"I would like to have a different room; this one was not to my liking," I said sternly.

"I'm very sorry, sir. Was it something specific?" he asked.

"No. Not really; I just didn't like the view."

"Here you go. Take this room; it has a better view, sir."

"Thank you. You've been very helpful," I said.

Here I was in the middle of an overthrow of the U.S. government, and I was not checking into an arranged room that could be bugged. By changing rooms, I felt like I could talk to Cindy with no fear of being spied upon. I needed to talk to her and see how things were at home. I settled down in my new room and called Cindy. The phone rang only once and she answered, "Oh, Adam. I'm so glad you called. I'm on pins and needles here, and I was worried about you. Is everything okay? The kids are at friend's houses, and I'm here alone, and I want to know when to tell the kids, and . . ."

"Calm down," I said. "Everything is fine. Nothing will happen until Monday. The military will make its move, and I will address the nation that evening. I suggest you just let the kids watch it unfold and let them see me on the TV. The security will show up after I appear for the first time. Your phone will blow up, but you can handle it. I advise you to turn it off while you explain to the kids what is happening. They need to be careful and do what their bodyguards tell them."

Cindy replied, "I'm sorry, honey. I'm so nervous for you and the kids, but I will handle things here. Our parents are going to be in shock, but I'm going to tell them they can't get in touch with you for a few days."

"That's fine. Just tell them I will get in touch soon," I replied.

It was a long weekend waiting for Monday morning. The General said he would send a car for me at 0700 and move me to a safe place. I spent a lot of time thinking about how the people would accept his coup. At first I felt they would resent the fact that the military is doing something that had never been done in our country. Of course, we were formed as a constitutional republic a few years after the Revolutionary War in which we separated from England. But this was different because it looked as if we were throwing our democratic principles out the window for a dictatorship, which couldn't be further from the truth. However, the people wouldn't know that until they heard from me. I had no desire to be a dictator; I just wanted to fix problems swiftly with no negotiation.

Oh my, I guess that did sound like a dictator, but it wouldn't be like that in the end. They would have to trust me . . . Hell, now I sounded like a used car dealer. I needed some sleep!

Saturday morning turned into Saturday afternoon pretty quickly as I caught up on some much-needed rest. I was hungry, too. I didn't know who was picking up the tab on the room, but I was about to order room service. I ate a nice meal, took a hot shower, and settled into an easy chair to call and check in on Cindy. She answered her phone this time with a little less excitement, "Hello, honey. Everything is normal here. How about you?"

"Normal is not a word I will be using for a while," I said laughing.

"I didn't sleep well with you gone, but I'm resting today," She responded.

"I miss you already, and I don't know when I will see you for sure, but I'm definitely going to work it out ASAP," I said.

"I miss you, too, and I love you," Cindy whimpered.

"Don't cry. Everything will be okay. I promise. I love you. Get some rest."

We said our goodbyes and hung up. I watched a couple of football games in the room and took a walk to a restaurant close to the hotel. It might be the last time for quite a while that I would be able to walk somewhere by myself, no security or bodyguards. It made me wonder about the men or women that ran for President of the U.S. In the case of a man like Reagan, George W. Bush, Romney, Hillary, or Trump, they are rich and didn't need the headaches that come along with the job. For anyone with that kind of money, why would they want to complicate their lives? Was it for fame, power, or maybe their heart was really in the right place, and they truly thought they could help the country. My parents loved Reagan and had kind words to say about Bill Clinton. They felt Bush 43 was extremely unlucky to have 9/11 happen soon after he took office. But I never heard a kind word about Obama or Hillary. They felt like the country was way down the wrong path under Obama, who they viewed as someone who only wanted to be a rock star. Hillary seemed to be his under-study, and they voted for Trump with a great deal of anxiety. He wasn't going to be the normal guy in the White House. He was a mold breaker. His "Drain the Swamp" motto was brilliant. He fooled all the pollsters, but not me. I knew by the size of the crowds he was drawing at every campaign rally, that he would beat Hillary and by more than people thought. I was glad to see him win. I hoped he would be able to work across the aisle, but that would not happen due to the radical left wing of the Democrat party. Their Socialist ideas and approach to taxation and government control would constantly be contrary to President Trump's vision of America. Herein lies the problem that exists today. Under President Obama, the Republicans in Congress obstructed his agenda at every turn. Apply common sense here. If obstructing Obama was the wrong thing to do, why didn't Hillary Clinton win the election in 2016? Think about that. The American people confirmed (by not voting for Hillary) that the obstruction was warranted and the right thing to do. Obama's plan to "fundamentally change America" was not what the majority of *states* wanted; notice I said "states", NOT popular vote. Our constitution protects the smaller states from being dominated by the larger populated east and west coast states. Now the Democrats felt obliged to obstruct President Trump at every turn. They didn't seem interested in compromise, which suited me fine. I have said many times in my life in coaching, teaching, business, and government circles that if you keep doing what you're doing, you're going to keep getting what you're getting! I've applied that concept when people were unhappy with losing and failing. I believe you must try something different or work harder and longer, but don't just stay in the rut that keeps you in the same miserable place. That is why Donald Trump was elected President of the U.S. in 2016. People wanted to try something completely different, and, well..they got it. Never before has an elected President worked as hard as Trump, and never before have so many worked so hard to get rid of him. Nothing he has done or will do in the future, will be accepted by the Democrats. Their goal is to impeach him and have him convicted in the Senate and thrown out of office. Their actions just proved to me that the Democrats feared success from Trump's agenda and knew that they would not be able to regain the power of the office of the Presidency in the near future. They would rather see the country fail at foreign relations, the economy, immigration, and at keeping our military strong. This was the liberal strategy. I saw through the Democrats' antics a long time ago, which lead me to form a strong opinion about compromise. Common sense should tell anyone that if there is a problem to solve, there is a right and a wrong answer. Why would I take the right answer and water it down by including part of the wrong answer and then not solve the problem? Republicans and Democrats have "compromised" for many years. This process ended up "kicking the can down the road" and solves nothing. Both parties threw money at the problem and we've ended up $22 trillion in debt. Obama ran our debt up over $10 trillion, more than doubling it. This was more than all other Presidents combined! You must use the right answer to solve a problem and don't accept any foolish compromise just to satisfy the other party. At least you would find out which side is best to lead the country and everyone would benefit. Based on what I'd seen from President Trump, he has the right ideas, but will get *zero* cooperation. So which party was right to obstruct? The answer was plain as the nose on my face. The Republicans won the 2016 election by obstructing, and the Democrats were making fools of themselves for obstructing Trump.

The liberal, socialist leaning, far left of the Democrat party had brought on what was about to happen on Monday.

Chapter 6

IT BEGINS

called Cindy on Sunday morning just to say hello and tell her that I loved her. I looked forward to the NFL games in the afternoon. I wasn't going to be able to watch my Green Bay Packers, but I would be able to catch the updates and highlights while I watched the regionally televised game. The local game was Washington vs. Dallas. At least I could root for the Redskins, since I despised the Cowboys. The game took my mind off events coming Monday morning. I even fell asleep during the second half for a much-needed nap. I woke up to find out the Packers won, as did the Cowboys. Not perfect, but I'd take it.

I spent the rest of the evening writing my prepared statement for the press. It wasn't hard. I wrote a novel based on everything I believed and would say much of the same Monday night. I just hoped I could overcome my nerves and come across like I had some intelligence. I did get a little sleep, but 0700 Monday morning came quickly. I was taken to a command center and all the military men saluted me as I walked in. I knew to salute them back and show the respect that I truly had for the men and women in uniform. I would watch everything unfold on a TV screen just like most Americans would. At 0900, Operation New Dawn launched! Tanks rolled up blocked off streets to the White House as troops were deployed throughout the city. Jets flew over the capitol in a show of force. General St. Claire issued a statement to all television networks describing the situation and declaring martial law. Everyone was told to go about their business as usual, but that there would be a curfew of 7:00 p.m. est. that night so that the entire nation could be addressed as to what was happening and what the future held.

The first network to report was CNN. The newscaster reported, "Never before in our nation's history has our military or any faction of it engaged in a concerted action against its own leadership. As leading members of the Army, Marines, Navy, Air Force, and other military bodies secure control of Washington, D.C., we are getting reports of minimal violence, zero casualties, and maximum public cooperation. Indeed, according to some reports, and eruption of cheers arose as the President was removed from the White House earlier this afternoon. Meanwhile, rumors have been circulating about who exactly is in charge of this historic revolution."

It seemed that people were so shocked they just fell right into line with very few problems arising from the city occupation. They needed more information. They didn't know who to blame, who to be mad at, or which side started this coup. They just knew the President was 'fired' along with everyone in Congress. Neither Republicans nor Democrats got preferential treatment. Only after my speech at 1930 hours would they begin to understand. I was the Commander-in-Chief now, so I've converted to military time. (Ha-ha)

My old friend Craig from the FBI showed up to take me to the White House. I greeted him with a hearty, "Hello. It's nice to see the guy who got me into this."

Craig smiled and laughed and said, "It's an honor to see you again. I'm your ride to the White House."

"Good deal," I said. "Let's get going."

On the ride over, I saw the military presence deployed around the city. It was intimidating to say the least. I am glad all citizens had followed the directives so far, and were waiting to hear from whoever was in charge. Craig escorted me all the way to the oval office. He wished me luck and left. General St. Claire appeared in the doorway and said, "The press room will be ready in 15 minutes."

"Okay," I answered.

General St. Claire asked, "You ready? This is your moment, Mr. Marsh."

I answered, "It's not all about me; it's about the country."

The General smiled, "Well, let's just say you're about to become a lot more well known. I'll see you in the press room."

The General turned to leave, but I interrupted, "I've been thinking a lot about your plan."

The General turned back to face me, "And . . ."

I replied, "You chose wisely, General. I've always been an honorable man. I've been fair in my dealings and generous to my loved ones and neighbors. Loyal to the people I care about, and if I were in your position I'd have asked me, too."

The General put on a wide grin, "I'm glad we're in agreement about your qualifications."

"But," I asked, "what if the public doesn't accept me in this role? What if I'm destined to be a celebrity but *not* a commander?"

The General laughed and said, "Well then, you and Barrack Obama will have something in common."

That made me laugh out loud, but the General continued, "Many people will object to you. They will do so out of fear. Fear of our power. Fear of change. Fear of new ideas. It's only natural. So, the important thing is: The people have to see benefits RIGHT AWAY. There can be no lag period. If we are to revolt, then we must do so at a tangible level. None of this

"Obamacare" nonsense, where they put up a website built in 1992.

I laughed out loud again.

General St. Claire continued, "Trust will come when the tide turns for the better, Commander Marsh. For now, though, it's on you to do something important." The General turned to go out the door again and said, "Give 'm one hell of a speech!"

I was alone with my thoughts for a few moments. There was no turning back now. I was about to be introduced as the leader of the United States of America, not a President, but the Commander in Chief.

I would be the leader of the free world. I would have power beyond my imagination. "Power corrupts, and absolute power corrupts absolutely." But I know how power should be handled, and I must prove it to all the US citizens. My mouth is so dry, and my nerves are starting to affect me. I have to keep it together. I must find some water and take a deep breath.

My time had arrived.

Chapter 7

NOW, IT'S MY TURN

The pressroom was busting at the seams with reporters and cameras. General St. Claire stepped up to the podium. All eyes of the press looked up at him; their notepads, tape recorders, and cameras at the ready. General St. Claire began, "Before I introduce our new Commander-in-Chief, I'd like to take a moment to thank the press corps for their honest and straightforward reporting of today's events. Lord knows if the Obama administration were still in power, the military's actions on this day would be spun as an act of domestic terrorism. Quite the contrary; however, we are not terrorists. We are proud and patriotic Americans. And our new Commander-in-Chief will be pleased to explain our position in greater detail."

The entire audience stirred with anticipation.

General St. Claire continued, "So without further ado, I introduce to you . . ." Cameras at the ready, recorders at the ready, notepads at the ready, "Commander Adam Marsh.

A great stir swept across the room. A moment went by. The General viewed the room's doorway. But then, after another moment, I walked in, smiling and confident. I replaced the General at the podium. Cameras flashed. Whispers came from all directions.

I began to speak, "Allow me to echo the General's gratitude about the press' graceful use of the First Amendment. I hope that if I ever do anything unpopular, you will be equally candid in your evaluations." I looked at the General. He nodded. I gave a quick nod back, then looked out at the press again. I continued, "Our country has been in enormous trouble for quite some time now. Congress spent years operating with an abysmal approval rating, and yet, despite the heartfelt complaints of the American people, we failed to do what we knew was truly necessary. We failed to rise-up, go to the polls, and clean house.

Reporters' hands moved FURIOUSLY upon their pads.

I continued, "This will not be an uprising defined by violence. Nor is it a transition away from democracy. What it is, is more akin to an intervention. We're here—*temporarily*—to straighten things out. After which point we'll be more than pleased to step back and welcome the old way of doing things. But know this: When I say 'the old way of doing things,' I don't mean how it's been in the immediate past. I mean how it was when the nation was growing, both economically and in terms of its great moral character.

One female reporter raised her hand.

I continued, "I'll take your questions in just a moment. First, just some basic points about what the American people can expect in the near-term. For starters, as of now, we are in a state of martial law. All communities, from the major urban centers to our proud small towns will be graced with a military presence. Yet there will be No checkpoints. NO restraints upon the normal activities of your day-to-day lives. In fact, should any of our military officers become courageous and begin to interfere with the ordinary flow of your lives, you are to report them to us at the White House right away. They WILL be eliminated from their posts. In addition, I am known now as the Commander-in-Chief. That does not mean I am your President. This distinction is drawn because America has a proud tradition of *electing* its leaders, and sometimes the ones we vote for are actually the ones who win."

The press corps laughed.

I continued, "So seeing as I have been appointed by our military, I am formally fit to lead them. And since they are our nation's current leaders, then—yes— it can be said that, FOR NOW, I am the nation's leader.

I continued, "However, know this: The most tangible changes in the American people's lives will relate to *money*. These monetary changes will surface soon. To be sure, there will be ideological shifts, as well, but no one in our nation is expected to agree with them. This is not, and shall never be, a kingdom. That being said, the changes we have in mind shall be implemented for the betterment of ALL."

The members of the press corps all began to chatter. Nodding, I pointed over at the female reporter who first raised her hand a moment ago. I said, "Yes? You—"

She stood, "Commander Marsh—"

I stopped her, "No, no, no. The military personnel call me commander. I expect the American people to call me Mr. Marsh or just Adam if you like. I've answered to much worse in my life," I laughed.

The female reporter said, "Okay, Adam . . ."

I smiled and nodded.

"What exactly are the changes we can expect? I mean, surely there must be some kind of plan—."

I nodded again and said, "The plan is a detailed and straightforward one. In fact, it's the very same plan that the American people have read about in my book. Now don't be afraid as you read it. Remember it is fiction. But it does contain many ideas we will be following. Next question," I said.

Every single reporter raised his/her hand and said my name at the same time. I finally got them to settle down, as I called on one of the male reporters most critical of President Trump. He began, "I'm not a bit upset that you have essentially fired President Trump, but I'm not quite sure I understand whose side you're on."

"Let me stop you there for a moment, I declared. "I'm firmly on the side of the people of this great nation. I intend to affect change swiftly, without argument or discussion."

"Then you will operate as a dictator, I presume?" he chided.

"Yes. If that is the label you choose, then so be it. The point is that decisions will be made that affect changes without going through red tape. This is a dictatorship, but I will be a benevolent Dictator, and you will make your mind up on that based on the results of my actions. And I welcome that," I replied.

"This won't sit well with the people," he claimed. "They will never accept this."

I replied, "Once again, I beg you, don't prejudge or label me. I don't want to be a dictator or labeled that way. I'm the guy the military chose to lead them and the American people for a short period of time. Our goal is to fix this mess the politicians have made. I'm just a guy with the answers that had no way to get my point across. Neither side would do what has to be done under normal circumstances. What was I to do, go to my congressman and lay it all out for him or her? He or she would have called for security to take me to jail and charged me with treason. Even if my ideas were put before Congress, there would have been zero cooperation as we have seen for the last 20 years." I paused and raised both my hands to have all the reporters take a seat, and I said, "This press conference is finished. I know you have a million questions, but you can wait until tomorrow when things begin to unfold. Goodnight."

I headed back to the oval office to meet with General St. Claire.

"Damn, you're good," he stated, as I took my seat. "You were born for this. You could not have been any more clear with those reporters. I loved it. We are going to do great things."

"I sure hope so, but what about my family? Are they under protective custody?" I asked.

"Yes," the General replied, "they are safe and tucked away in a secret location."

"My kids aren't going to like that much, but Cindy is handling that end of it," I said. I realized I would sleep in the White House that night. It was amazing and surreal.

It was winter in D.C., and the grounds were bleak and well lit. As I gazed out the window, I thought about the people who had stood in this exact spot and contemplated their next move. Thinking about the rich history of the Oval Office and its occupants over the years, was overwhelming. Never in my wildest dreams could I have ever imagined I would be standing in the office of the leader of the free world. The rug in the middle of the room with the Presidential Seal of the United States had been walked on by world leaders. As a history teacher, I had a great deal of appreciation for where I was about to conduct business. I would be a part of history for this great nation. I had to do a good job. I had to make this work.

Chapter 8

FLASHBACKs

could only guess that people wondered how a high school history teacher/ construction business owner could ever write a novel. I really had no idea that I could; I just knew I wanted to--needed to--do or write something to wake up the people of this country. To wake them up to the fact that the gridlock we were experiencing was killing our nation. I remembered the day I decided to sit down and string together some pages. Twelve hours later, I had 40 pages. The English language was butchered in those pages, but I could find someone to help me correct all that. It only took me about two months to finish it. It was wintertime and construction was a little slow at the time, so I took advantage of my free time. Of course, with a family, life got in the way, and getting the book in a proper form to present to a publisher was a whole 'nother ball of wax.

Flashback—

I was sitting in my home office in front of my computer, furiously writing away (on my legal pad). After several moments, I paused and looked toward the door. I yelled, "Cindy!" No answer. "Cindy?"

Cindy yells back, "What?!"

"You have to come in here. NOW!"

I heard her footsteps rushing up the stairs and toward the office. Then Cindy entered, out of breath. She said, "What? Is everything alright?"

I replied, "Everything's fine. Everything's GREAT." I looked her in the eye. "I think I might have a best-seller on my hands."

She rolled her eyes and smiled, collected her breath and said, "Adam, sweetie, every beginning author thinks that. Step one is *finishing* the book and actually getting it published."

I grabbed her playfully and put her in my lap and scolded, "Thanks for the positive reinforcement. Ever think about coaching? (sarcastically) You'd be great!"

She pinched me playfully and laughed. She inquired, "When *will* it be finished?"

"Very soon," I replied, "but I have some time to kill. You want to fool around?" She jumped up out of my lap and smiled, "No. I mean yes, but no; I have to pick the kids up after practice."

"Never hurts to ask," I joked. "Just know this," I added, "whether one person reads this novel or a million people do, our lives could really change."

Cindy gave me a loving look, nodded, and walked away.

Flashback—

I stood near a printer that was running off copy after copy of my completed book manuscript. As I watched the pages being produced by the machine, one of my employees, Marcus, a black man in his mid-40s, entered my room.

Marcus asked, "What's goin' on here, Mr. Marsh?"

"It's my book. I finally finished last night."

Curious, Marcus stepped over to the machine and stood next to me. Marcus said, "Man, I didn't know you were a writer."

"Me neither. But I am now," I replied.

Marcus looked at the growing stack of pages and asked, "What is it about?"

I hesitated for a moment, then answered, "It's about America. It's fiction though. The character in it, he's a regular guy, just like you or me. But he wants changes. And he starts a revolution. And makes the changes come true."

Marcus' eyes widen a little. He nodded, clearly thinking his boss was nuts. Marcus asked, "What, um, kinds of changes, Mr. Marsh?"

I started, "Well, first of all . . . uh, maybe you should just wait and read it for yourself. I don't want to spoil it for you."

Flashback—

Wearing a suit and tie, I sat in the company of Alexander Nance, a famous conservative talk show host. He was in his 60's with gray hair and bifocals that he looked over the top of when he addressed me. He needed them to read his notes that rested in his lap with his legs crossed. The studio looked like a library in someone's home with big, comfortable chairs. If not for the cameras and lights, I would have thought he asked me to stop by his house to talk for a while.

I was in the middle of a serious interview and I continued, "Yes, I'd want to fire Congress."

Alexander Nance asked, "Just fire 'm, huh?"

I answered, "Oh, yes. Unfortunately, we're in a state of emergency in this country. We can't just wait around for them to be voted out. In my America, I'll be walking into Congress like Donald Trump on "The Apprentice" and I'm going to look out over the crowd and say, "You're fired.""

Nance cracked up laughing. Nance confirmed, "I love it. I'd pay to see that. What else?"

"The President, too. President Obama has to go. And the Supreme Court Justices. All three branches will be eliminated."

"So, anarchy, in other words?"

I replied, "Only temporarily. And besides, Mr. Nance, does what we have right now not resemble anarchy?"

The host smiled a bit, then nodded.

I was on a roll and said, "In addition, there will be no government housing provided for any person unless he or she can pass a drug test. By the same rationale, no person shall receive food stamp entitlements without passing a drug test. And when a person has the misfortune of becoming unemployed, the benefits provided to him or her by the government will only last for six months - straight and clean. Then, you're on your own. Go get a job."

Nance joked, "Does that go for the President, too? Will he get unemployment benefits?"

I laughed, but said, "Not that he deserves them or anything, but yes. Equality needn't be thrown out the window. The President can have his six months, too. Then he's out. And the Affordable Care Act goes right with him. Just like a regular employee has to clear out his locker upon termination, this guy has to take home his bad ideas."

Nance rejoiced, "I sense our viewers are enjoying this very much."

"Thank you."

Nance responded, "And from what I recall in reading your book, there's a religious component, as well . . ."

I confirm, "Absolutely. Nothing to be ashamed of there. We put the Ten Commandments in our school curriculum. After all, those teachings have guided humanity's moral compass for thousands of years – no sense in keeping them away from our classrooms."

"And . . . nativity scenes?"

I told him, "I'll be allowing them on government property. This doesn't mean I'll be ending the separation of church and state; I'll just be reinstituting a shred of common sense. I mean, we have the words "In God We Trust" printed on our currency, and nobody complains about that. So, I'll be re-allowing this proud part of our heritage in government buildings. If people don't want to participate in it - Fine. They can stay home, or just keep their eyes shut."

Nance looked astonished and said, "You know, I'm listening to you talk here, and it sounds like you have actual plans. You keep referring to what *you* will do, in real life, when I should remind those watching at home that this is just make believe. It's a novel."

I sheepishly said, "Yes. Thank you, Mr. Nance. You're correct. My wife catches me doing that all the time. We all know I'll never be in the White House. But we also know that whether they're in a fiction book or in a nonfiction book, IDEAS are very real things. And these are REAL ideas for the American people to chew on."

Nance nodded, briefly studying a hardback copy of *The (New) American Way*. Nance replied, "Indeed they are." He looked back at Adam. "And certainly not everybody will be thrilled with them!"

"Oh, you took the words right out of my mouth, Mr. Nance. I've met *several* people who are less than thrilled . . ."

Flashback –

In another suit and tie, I sat across from Susan Mercer, the host of a popular liberal talk show, on one of the mainstream media news channels.

Susan Mercer speaks. "I just don't see how these ideas can ever become really popular . . ."

I stated, "Well, forgive me, but they already have, Mrs. Mercer. We're selling tens of millions of copies—"

"Yes, but, for instance: Having people have to pass DRUG TESTS to get on food stamps or in public housing? I mean, it's entertaining as a conservative fantasy, but—"

I interjected, "It's more than entertaining, ma'am. It points to a long-standing problem."

"Which is what?"

I respond, "Do you actually enjoy paying your taxes? You think it's efficient to do so? Simple?"

"No, but-"

I push some more, "So, why keep cooperating? I don't understand."

Mercer answered sternly, "Because it helps people! It's generous. It's a civic duty!"

I asked, "Where's this mysterious 'help' you speak of? I mean, I don't know about you, but after I pay my taxes, I don't receive an invoice showing me what I've paid for. The government ends up doing whatever in the world they want to with my money. And be that as it may, it's generous of ME to be offering them about half of what I make. Nice and clean. Take it, guys! Do your best with it."

Mercer sighed and shook her head. She claimed, "You're quite an opinionated man, Mr. Marsh."

I replied, "Well, hopefully your viewers have listened to some of my opinions."

Flashback—

I walked into the movie studio in Hollywood. In semi-casual clothes, I sat on a couch across from a reception desk outside of a corner office. I thumbed through a magazine. After a moment, the receptionist walked over. She said, "He's ready for you."

I said with surprise, "Oh, wow. That was fast." I slapped the magazine down on the coffee table and got up to follow the receptionist toward the office.

The receptionist lowering her voice said, "He's been really excited to meet you."

Together we walked toward the door. As it opened, the receptionist guided me inside. I found myself standing in front of my favorite actor and director, Clint Eastwood.

Behind the desk were posters of some of his great movies: *Unforgiven* and *Million Dollar Baby* were given the most prominent positions. It seems he is more proud of his directorial prowess than his acting, but of course he had acting roles in both movies. The room had no windows, so there was a lot of space for many posters of *Josey Wales* and *Dirty Harry. The Good, the Bad, and the Ugly* had the wall behind me covered. I couldn't help looking at all these posters while Mr. Eastwood watched me turn completely around in front of him.

Walking over, I said, "Sir, I am so excited to meet you—"

Eastwood responded, "Sit down. None of that 'sir' stuff."

I was star struck, but managed to say, "Oh, of course." I took a seat.

Eastwood professes, "I'm not here much, so I'm not the decorator. My staff put all these posters up so I wouldn't forget the things I've done. I'm getting old and forgetful, and they think this will help." We both have a little chuckle and he continues, "That was a pretty good book you wrote there, kid."

I answered, "Oh, thank you, s--, I mean, Mr. Eastwood."

Clint conveyed, "I'll be honest with you: It moved me to tears. And I'm not a man who cries too easy. Know what I mean?"

"Well, I—um—hope I didn't upset you."

Clint jokes, "Upset me? You're kidding? You inspired me to my core. My wife had to rock me in her arms for hours."

I had to laugh a little at that. Picturing Dirty Harry being rocked in his wife's arms was too much!

"I want the movie rights, kid. *Now*. I'm concerned, however."

"Concerned about . . . what?"

"That they're not available anymore. You probably sold them right away for more than I could ever afford."

I divulge, "No, no, no. They're fine. They're available! Very available. To be honest, most of your colleagues weren't really interested. They're a little too liberal, if you know what I mean."

"No kidding. Bunch of softies, those guys. But I think there's a blockbuster hit awaiting us here . . ."

I nodded my head and thought to myself, I must be dreaming. I wrote this book to become a movie. I thought more people would see the movie than would read the book. I wanted it to reach the most possible citizens of this country to get my point across; gridlock is killing this nation along with debt and socialist ideas. It was always meant to be presented to Mr. Eastwood to become his movie project.

My dream is becoming a reality!

Chapter 9

BACK TO REALITY

All the military personnel who briefed me initially sat around a large oak table. I entered the room in a freshly ironed suit. This time I greeted them as their leader, not as a civilian. They all rose and waited for me to take a seat. When I sat, they sat.

I announced, "Okay. First things first—"

General St. Claire leaned forward and said, "We need to start winning battles, not just fighting them."

All the men nodded, except for me.

"Sir, in recent times, this nation has developed a habit of beginning military campaigns, and then losing the stomach—the fortitude—to carry them all the way to the end. This has to stop. We've got unfinished business in Iraq, Syria, and Afghanistan—"

I interrupted, "Excuse me, General—."

The General stopped speaking. Awkwardness hits the room like a bucket of ice water.

"No confusion at all. I'm just explaining to you a long-standing probl—"

I cut him off saying, "Okay, then. Good. No confusion. I happen to agree with your assessment. I don't like seeing military waste either. But first things first: We have to institute a *gradual unrolling* of our plan. Otherwise, people will think we're insane."

General St. Claire, with a serious look on his face, responded, "With all due respect, sir, many of them already do."

It was the icebreaker I needed. I smiled and said, "Fair enough. Which is why this first phase of activity will be milder than what they may be expecting. We have to inspire their confidence; otherwise, who's to prevent some other group from overthrowing *us*?"

The General cleared his throat and answered, "That's a reasonable point, sir. Just don't forget: We *are* the U.S. military."

I smiled gently, and then nodded in agreement. I added, "So let's hang on to that privilege, shall we?"

Sighing slightly, General St. Claire nodded back.

Then I stood up and started to circle the table. I began, "What I propose at the current juncture is a three-point plan. New rules and regulations. Number one; there will be no more extended unemployment benefits. They will soon be a thing of the past, and someday people will hear about that concept and laugh their butts off."

The men around the table grinned and nodded.

I continued, "Now, this doesn't mean people will get cut off right away. They will all get one more check. *One last chance.* Then the benefits are effectively discontinued. As for regular benefits, they will continue to last for 26 weeks, just as the system was originally designed to provide for."

The men nodded.

I continued, "Number two, one can no longer attain regular unemployment benefits, welfare, food stamps, or disability if one does not pass a drug test. This one's very important. You want benefits, then be a clean, respectable person. Don't pour government money into your addiction."

One lieutenant spoke up, "Amen!"

I finished, "Number three, we temporarily *suspend* our long-held freedom of assembly! I will hear no dissent at this point in time. Not while we're under Martial Law." I had to take a moment to catch my breath. My face was red with passion. "When is the next press conference?" I asked.

General St. Claire responded, "You are the Commander-in-Chief. You can call a press conference for 0300 hours in the morning and the room will be full."

I commanded, "Call one for this evening at 1900. After we release this 3-point agenda, I will need to calm a few people down."

General St. Claire said, "I will make it so."

I inquired, "General, do I have a personal assistant position open? If so, I'd like to get one ASAP."

"Is there someone you have in mind, or do you want me to send someone from our ranks?"

"One of yours is fine. Also, call the President's cabinet together for a meeting at 1100 hours this morning. These people aren't politicians, so I might get along with them. But do send a security detail to help set the mood."

The General said, "Right away."

I went to the oval office. I prepared some notes for the cabinet meeting. I had to keep the country running smoothly and wait for my changes to take effect. This is a critical meeting, so I can't mess it up. I hoped they would buy in to what I was trying to do. If not, this could get ugly. The time flew by and 1100 hours came upon me. I walked into the cabinet meeting room to find every chair filled and five military security personnel. All eyes were on me as I took my seat. This was day two of the takeover. Information was at a premium and I was the only one handing it out.

I began, "Thank you for coming. I know you are wondering how something like this could happen in our country, but I promise you, it is for the best. You are about to have input with me, the new Commander-in-Chief, and I can make a decision based on that input that can be implemented without delay and without having to argue with Congress."

Most of the participants smiled broadly, yet some still looked a little reluctant. I continued, "I recognize most of you and I would love to know each of you on a personal level, but for now I will just use your title. We will be meeting again tomorrow, so don't plan on going anywhere. I'm sure you've already seen the three-point plan to start saving money. This affects only one of you. Make it happen. Put in the proper procedures and do not fail. Other changes are coming, but I need you to keep the status quo until I issue an order that affects your department. Tell everyone you deal with that the U.S. is just doing some house cleaning internally, so don't panic and do something you'll regret. I will handle problem individuals with extreme measures. These individuals will learn not to task me! If you have a problem you can't handle, bring it to me and we will solve it together."

Everyone there seemed to be in agreement. I hated to ask if there were any questions. I was sure there were, but I cut them off at the pass. I said, "I know you have questions, but I have to meet with another group now. Notice, I only fired the President, Congress, and the Supreme Court. I kept all of you. The President and I agree on most things, but he couldn't get things done under the previous system. My system works quickly and decisively. Follow my lead, help me, and I will help you make the country work properly again. We will meet tomorrow at the same time. I will answer any questions then."

There were no outbursts or arguments. Maybe the security detail had something to do with that.

I went back to the oval office. I needed some lunch, but it needed to be a working lunch. About that time, in walks General St. Claire with a soldier in tow. "Commander," he said, "I would like to introduce your first personal assistant, Lieutenant Jerry Mathis."

I smiled and responded, "You sound as if there might be a second one in the future. Are you setting up this young man for failure?" Everyone is laughing, as the General replied, "Why no. Just stating the obvious. I doubt you've ever had one before."

Jerry looked nervous, and stood a half step behind the General. He was short, about 5'7", and already had thinning hair. I suspected he had long since completed basic training in the army, and looked a little out of shape. That's what sitting behind a desk all day will do to a person.

"How old are you and where are you from, Jerry?" I asked.

"I'm 26 and from Kentucky," he replied. "Beaver Dam to be exact."

"You'll do fine and thank you, General."

The General left and I turned to Jerry and said, "Your first order will be to visit the White House Chef in the kitchen and bring us back some lunch with a big Diet Coke. We will eat in the oval office where it's quiet and we can discuss a few things."

"Yes, sir," he said. "Anything in particular?"

"Surprise me."

Jerry left nervously, probably wondering if he could pick something I would like. I stopped long enough to call Cindy and check on her and the kids, letting them know everything is going fine. They will be able to watch the events unfold on TV.

Jerry came through the door as I hung up the phone. He carried a tray with two cheeseburgers, two small plates of fries, and two soft drinks. I started to laugh and said, "Wow, you went way out on a limb there with your choice!" He smiled and shook his head.

I thought, "I like this kid; he has potential."

Chapter 10

IMPLEMENTING POLICY

The 1900 hour press conference rolled around quickly. Once again it was a full house. I had called this one for only one reason: To educate the press and the politicians on one thing—taxation. I walked in after being introduced by General St. Claire and I welcomed everyone. All the usual attendees were hanging on my every word. So, I began, "I've asked you here tonight to drive one point across to each and every American. We absolutely CANNOT continue to spend money like a drunken sailor - my apologies to our Naval personnel. The U.S. government is $22 trillion in debt, and we are adding to that at a break-neck pace. IT HAS TO STOP! As you see my plan unfold for our country, you will see that almost everything I do will save our government money in the long run.

There will be no more kicking the can down the road, no more argument, no more government shutdowns, and a tax system that makes sense. Money makes the world go 'round, and we have to borrow too much of ours. This is what I want you to learn."

I had Jerry bring out displays. I felt like I was back in the classroom. I had a laser and pointed at the top of the page. It is a paragraph from a *Forbes* article about the number of billionaires in the U.S. It says there are 540 billionaires with a total combined wealth of approximately $2.4 trillion. These were statistics from 2016. The numbers change almost daily, but not by enough to change my point. Most liberals, socialists, and many poor people think you can fix all our problems by taxing the rich. My job was to explain why that won't work. I started by saying, "Let's say this year, we add $1 trillion to the deficit, meaning we spend $1 trillion more THIS YEAR than we take in. We already have a sliding scale tax that the richer people pay at the highest rate. Can we raise it even more, like some socialists want? How about 70%? Well, let's pretend we tax them at 100% of everything they own. The government seizes all they own and all their money. We know they have $2.4 trillion, but we have to liquidate everything and who is left to purchase everything these billionaires own? The government created a $1 trillion deficit with a 37% tax rate on these people for their income for that year. The $2.4 trillion you got by taking everything they own will cover the most recent deficit and retire about 6.4% of our national debt. Who will the government pick on the next year? The billionaires are broke so we have to move down the ladder, but those rich people have even less and without the billionaires paying at least their 37%, the deficit will be even larger next year. Do you understand that the scenario I just used is typical of Socialism and Communism? The governments in these systems run out of other people's money. You end up with shared misery for the entire population, except, of course, the high government officials. They never think the rules apply to them. There is only one-way to stop this from happening in our country: Stop spending more than you take in through taxation. We must stop wasting money. We must think about the future of our children and their children. And this is exactly my intention. I will cut out wasteful spending and pay down our national debt. And everyone is going to help and no one is exempt."

I didn't see too many reporters anxious to ask a question after that lecture. By the time I was done, I was breathing fire. "Before I take any questions," I asked, "is there anyone in the room who disagrees with anything said in this scenario?"

No one dared raise a hand. That was good. I had their attention. "Now are there any questions other than "How are you going to pay off the debt and rein in our budget deficits?"" I inquired.

Almost all the reporters nodded in the affirmative.

"It's already started and you will just have to report on it as it takes place. The next thing on my agenda is immigration. It is a broken system that will be fixed within the year," I proclaimed.

The hands flew up all over the room and the noise was deafening. I knew this would get them fired up, but, of course, this subject always does. I looked to call on one of the reporters, and I heard several questions being yelled at me at the same time, "Are you going to build a wall? Are you going to separate children from their parents? Are you going to give the "Dreamers' citizenship?" I held up both hands and said, "Okay, wait just a minute. I heard four or five different questions, and I would just like to say this: All of the things you want to know will be addressed. Common sense will solve every one of these problems. Problem one is illegal crossings. I will solve this with a wall of my choosing. It worked for Israel and it will work for us. The cost of the wall is approximately $25 billion. Every study I have seen says we spend anywhere from $100-$200 billion per year on illegal immigration. The answer to the problem lies in the simple math just presented. If you argue walls don't work or are too costly, you are just showing your ignorance. And I will add one more thing: Is one human life worth $25 billion?

I pause and give a very serious, stern look at the reporters, and say "Be careful how you answer that. Can you put a price on human life? I can introduce you to several people who have lost loved ones to illegal immigrants and you can give them your answer. And what about the harm to the illegal children, and deaths of the illegals themselves, what is their price tag? We must keep the criminal element out of our country, not to mention terrorists, who come across our southern borders. Keeping drugs from coming across the border will be a high priority. A huge amount of drugs comes through our gates, and we need more technology and officers to catch these criminal transporters. Once the wall is complete we will round up all the illegals and put them on the other side of that wall and they won't be coming back. However, I will be granting new green cards and a path to citizenship for the Dreamers. They are here by no fault of their own; it just makes good sense. I am not against legal immigration and the process needs to be streamlined and made less expensive. I intend to make all these things happen very soon. I hope that's enough for you reporters to write about for a while. I'm going to get to work and we will have another press conference later. Thank you."

I left the pressroom and headed back to the oval office. The General followed me in. He smiled and said, "You are absolutely fearless. The way you handle yourself around the press is just a beautiful thing to watch. I'm so glad we picked you to do this!"

"Thank you, General," I said, "but I might drive you crazy before this is over. I told Cindy I could do this in a year, so I'm in a hurry. Let's meet at 0700 tomorrow here in the conference room."

"Good by me," said General St. Claire. "See you in the morning."

The General left and Jerry came in the room. I told him to be there in the morning for the meeting and to get some rest. I needed to call Cindy.

Chapter 11

DAY 3

D ay 3 of the takeover started early for me. I woke up at 0400, and I had a lot on my mind. I wanted to get some things started that might take a while to complete, so I made a list of things to discuss at the 0700 meeting. Quiet time alone is the best time to think; I just need coffee. I slipped down to the kitchen in a sweat suit and find the coffee left over from the night shift security guards. It was black and strong, just the way I liked it. After a couple of hours, I dressed for the day and heard a knock on the door.

It was Jerry. "Do you need breakfast brought to you?"

"Yes," I said, "Make it three scrambled eggs, bacon and a glass of milk, and get yourself something."

"Okay. I will," answered Jerry. "Be back shortly."

We ate in a small conference room near my bedroom. Jerry finished and asked, "Is this an important meeting?"

"This is when I find out just how much of my book they have really read and are committed to implementing," I replied.

I walked into the large conference room and saw that all chairs were full and five security guards lined the walls. I took my seat and said, "The security personnel are excused and may leave the room. I don't think anyone in this meeting will try to harm anyone in the room. Guard the door while you wait outside."

Everyone just laughed a little as the guards left. General St. Claire looked at me and asked, "Are we going to talk about something they weren't supposed to hear?"

I simply reply, "Yes." There is a quiet anticipation in the room as I began.

"Gentlemen, I need your utmost attention," I demanded. Everyone looked intently at what I was about to say. "Okay. Here we go. First, I want to fix immigration. I want the Army Corps of Engineers, plus every sub-contractor that can work with them, to start building a 2000-mile wall, from the Pacific Ocean to the Gulf of Mexico. I don't want to hear any excuses about how there are certain areas that are too mountainous, or wet, or whatever. We are the finest builders in the world, with the smartest engineers and the most technology. I will not put up with any excuses.

The Chinese built a wall over 1000 years ago over all kinds of terrain. I think we can handle it. I have chosen the prototype for the wall. It will have steel slats on the bottom to solve the water drainage problems and to be able to see what is on the other side. The rounded top will have clips for razor wire. I want the illegal immigrants stopped cold."

General St. Claire clapped his hands and the rest of the room joined in. It made me feel great, but I might upset them with the next item on the agenda. General St. Claire was my right hand, and I turned to him and said, "General, I lean on you to delegate that to the right person and get them started building."

The General proudly responded, "Absolutely, Commander."

"Great," I replied. "Let's move on. The next thing is going to be tricky, but I know we can do this. I want our maximum security prisons cleaned out."

The General interrupted me and asked, "Where are we going to put them?"

I answered sternly, "In the ground!" I paused to watch their reaction and it was not positive. They mumbled among themselves for a few seconds and I said, "Let me explain before you express your opinion. First of all, I said maximum security, and that means the inmates are the worst of the worst. Does anyone in this room think any of these guys are going to become solid citizens some day? The sentence they received was not as harsh as it should have been. That is what is wrong with our justice system today. The punishment must deter the crime. Some liberal, activist judge had the prosecutor make a deal for a lighter sentence and avoided giving out the punishment the criminal deserved. And by the way, have any of you been inside a prison and seen what is going on there? It is nothing but factions carving out a niche and fighting each other for control of the prison 'economy.' They trade cigarettes for sexual favors or tattoos. I visited a medium security prison before writing my book and the warden told me the maximum-security prisons were much worse than the one I saw. This nation can't afford to provide food, shelter, water, electricity, healthcare, dental care, and guards to watch over them for *nothing* in return. I want this problem solved in this way: Go to the wardens and tell them we are moving their prisoners to a new location. Take them to a pre-arranged medical facility manned by Army, Navy, Air Force, National Guard, Marines, or Coast Guard doctors, sworn to secrecy. Sedate them, put them to sleep, harvest their organs, and have their bodies cremated. Catalogue and store the ashes until this operation is completed. This process must be kept totally secret. Have the wardens declare no visits while martial law is in effect. Catalog the organs with all vital information and start clearing the list of people waiting for an organ donor. This will be the last, best, and only thing these sorry individuals have ever done for society."

I clenched my jaw by this time and everyone knew I was serious. I could see that they could barely believe what they were hearing, but they seemed to know it made sense. "I think some of you may have skipped a chapter or two in my book. You should have known this was coming."

The General shook his head and said, "I knew it, and I still chose you."

"Then get things moving," I said, "and by the way, when the prison facility is empty, I want every homeless person rounded up in the area and given a place to live in the prison. The warden and guards will still have jobs, just a different clientele. The homeless can come and go as they please, and cell doors will remain unlocked unless the occupant wants that. At least these facilities will be trying to give a guy or girl a leg up to help them integrate back into the workforce and society in general. The guards will keep the peace and solve disputes."

The General looked around the room and announced, "After Commander Marsh ends this meeting, we will stay and decide on who to put in charge of each phase of these operations."

"Oh, I'm not done yet," I proclaimed. "Let's move on. I want a team of military men in full body armor to work in conjunction with every swat team in every city in America, to eliminate every gang. The SWAT teams know where every gang's territory lies, and I want them cleaned out. You are to use deadly force if necessary. If they have a firearm and don't disarm immediately when confronted, shoot to kill! Take them to the nearest civilian or military prison and lock them up. They have no rights under martial law. We will keep them as long as necessary. If they try to run, stop them any way you choose. I want all gang activity completely eliminated."

The General nodded in agreement and said, "We knew this wouldn't be easy, but it has to be done. We will get right on this."

"General, I would like to address the nation tonight at 1800 hours. Can you arrange that with the networks?" I asked.

Yes, Commander. I will make it so," the General answered.

I headed back to the oval office with Jerry in tow. As soon as I entered, I turned and sent Jerry to get the Secretary of State for me. He left and it was not long before the Secretary of State knocked on the door. He entered and asked, "What can I do for you Mr. President?"

"Oops" I said. "You're just used to saying that. You know better."

He started laughing with me and corrected himself, "Yes. I mean Commander Marsh."

The Secretary of State, Andrew Richey is the chief diplomat in the U.S. He is fifth in the line of succession to the presidency. I had heard he was used to the spotlight growing up, and did a little singing as a young man. He got along with others and handled himself well during negotiations with our allies. He had been having some health problems and was having trouble performing his duties. His knees had to be replaced a couple of years back, and he had gained a little weight he was still retaining. He never let that stop him from accomplishing his goals for the country. He has done a terrific job representing the U.S. throughout the world.

"Secretary Richey, I want you to tell me what problems are on the horizon worldwide."

"Commander Marsh," he began," the entire world is in shock watching what is happening in the U.S. Every leader of every nation I have been in contact with wants to know what's next. They are concerned about their relationship with the U.S. I reassured each leader that you just want everyone to honor all agreements and keep the peace."

"That's exactly what I wanted to hear," I answered, "and I hope that continues. I want the world to know this is a domestic housecleaning and that when it's over, we will be an even stronger country economically. Our ability to help keep the peace worldwide will be bolstered."

"I will pass this along to all countries. I'm sure they will appreciate it; well, most of them."

The secretary thanked me and left. Jerry took his place and asked, "Would you like some snacks or something to drink?"

"No," I answered. "Just get me the Secretary of Health and Human Services and the Secretary of Agriculture."

It wasn't long before they arrived. I greeted them at the door, "Secretary Latham and Secretary Kirkpatrick, have a seat." I walked behind my desk and sat across from them.

Secretary of Agriculture Matt Latham is a portly fellow, and always smells of tobacco smoke. I've been told he has a two pack a day cigarette habit. Of course the White House is a non-smoking area, now that I am residing there. If I keep him here for an extended period of time, he will probably get a little fidgety needing that nicotine fix. He and the Secretary of Health and Human Services, Christopher Kirkpatrick, are very good friends. However, Secretary Kirkpatrick's influence concerning good health hasn't rubbed off on Secretary Latham. Smoking is a terrible health hazard, and expensive in more ways than one. Don't smokers ever read the side of the cigarette package? I'm sure smokers are costing everyone big bucks in the health insurance pools. I've never had a single puff of a cigarette, and it continues to be one of my pet peeves. My newest pet peeve is the ACA, or Obamacare as most call it. Secretary Kirkpatrick will have to run interference for me when I do away with it.

"Gentlemen," I asked, "how are things in your part of the government?"

Sec. Latham spoke first, "I have made sure that each and every change you have instituted has been advertised on TV, radio, social media, and even bill-boards throughout the nation. There should be no rea-son for anyone to say, 'I didn't know.' Also we've sent out letters and left flyers at all government offices."

"Awesome, Secretary Latham," I proclaimed. "I couldn't ask for much more. Thank you, but you and I both know there will be a lot of backlash on these sub-jects. Both political parties have tried to cater to the poor by promising free food, housing, healthcare, cell phones, and money. All of these 'freebies' are offered with one catch, 'Vote for Me in the election, and the free stuff will continue.' In other words, the politi-cians are buying votes. And once again, none of these free things can be taken away, or so it seems. I can't name any entitlements that have been discontinued. We have to continue to take care of those incapable of taking care of themselves, BUT the perfectly fit and healthy people, who are gaming the system, have to be weeded out. We must change this entitlement culture. It has become a habit and habits can be broken. I can give you an example that relates to this conversation – about food stamps.

A man has a bird dog that is great at finding cov-eys of quail, but the dog is gun-shy. That means the dog runs off and hides at the sound of the gunshot, and the owner has to catch him to take him back home. This is unacceptable behavior and must be changed, or the dog is worthless as a hunter. So the man attempts to change this habit for the next few days by taking his gun with him to feed the dog. The man sets the dog's food bowl down, and as soon as the dog begins to eat, he fires the gun in the air. The dog runs into his house, and the man picks up the food and takes it back home. The next day, this exercise is repeated, and gets the same result. The third day, the man sets the food bowl down, and the dog begins to eat. The man fires his gun, but the dog remains at his bowl. The man fires again, and the dog continues to eat. Problem solved.

If the government takes away food stamps from the people gaming the system, when they get hungry enough, they will go to work, or starve. I'm betting they will get a job, buy their own food, and quit relying on the government. "

Sec. Latham smiles and says, "Great story and I agree with you. Habits can and must be broken in this instance. I will hold firm on requiring drug tests to be passed before handing out any entitlements. The abusers of the system will be purged from our rolls, and the authorities will be made aware of any violent protests."

I am impressed with Secretary Latham's dedication and proclaim, "Thank you again for your help and attitude on this very important process. Now, Secretary Kirkpatrick, let's attack your problem – Obamacare!"

Secretary Kirkpatrick spoke up, "The insurance companies are expecting the ACA to go away. They are preparing to return to the way things were before the Obama administration. Most people are confused and waiting to hear your solution to the healthcare dilemma. In fact, I'm rather curious myself."

"Secretary Kirkpatrick, let's brainstorm a bit on this subject," I said.

I began, "The middle class in America has been abused by Obamacare. Here's why: The middle class American family makes too much money to qualify for government subsidies but not enough money to pay premiums four times what they used to pay, and then get higher deductibles on top of that! The system was set up to force people to buy insurance at ridiculous prices, so the government could give free health care away to people who refused to work for it. Of course, the entire thing was a scam from the beginning. Nothing the Obama Administration said about this issue was true—about keeping your doctor, keeping your policy, or saving everyone money. So, what's happening today is the middle class can't pay their premiums, they have to drop the insurance and they become one of the uninsured statistics. Unless their employer furnishes their insurance, they have none. And even then, employers must require the employees to pay a higher portion of the premium than ever before - all because of Obamacare. And the thing that galls me the most is the part of Obamacare that requires companies that provide 'Cadillac' health insurance plans to their employees must pay a fine. Please tell me what degree of moron thought of this crap?" I was breathing fire again and the two Secretaries were looking at each other laughing. I took a deep breath and started laughing myself.

Secretary Latham spoke up, "I love your passion and your take on the entire situation. I have never felt so confident that the problems in this nation are about to be fixed."

Secretary Kirkpatrick chimed in, "I believe you have a handle on the situation. We are cheering for you."

"Cheering may not be enough," I answered, "but here is how I see this progressing from here forward." Secretary Kirkpatrick opens a notepad and starts writing. I continue,

"I have always believed in our free enterprise, capitalist system. The natural progression should go something like this: 1. Jobs are going to be plentiful after I deport all the illegal aliens." Eyebrows went up after this statement. "All the employers who provide health insurance will help reduce the number of uninsured people. 2. Wages will increase naturally in a tight job market. This will allow workers, not provided health insurance by employers to purchase their own policies. These policies will be more affordable with lower deductibles, and this time you can "keep your doctor" 3. Those who have policies under ACA now, and have a pre-existing condition, will get to keep these policies. The premiums will not be raised based on their condition. If they are unable to work, the government will pick up the tab. 4. We must educate those without health insurance to recognize that they are taking a serious risk. We have to make the uninsured understand that they must take responsibility for their own actions, or in this case, inactions. The government can't afford to give away health care; it is not a right. If it is the right of a citizen to have health care, why do doctors charge a fee for it from the individual? If it is a right, then doctors would all be working for, and paid by, the government. The only way a single payer healthcare system will work is if the government controls the cost of pharmaceuticals, the salaries of medical professionals, the number of doctors in each area of the country, the cost of hospital stays, surgery, etc. The doctors would not be able to pay back what it takes to make it through medical school in 100 years if they take out student loans. So the number of doctors and nurses would decrease drastically over time. Is this the system the liberal, socialist politicians want for our country? Maybe so, but the American people are smarter than that, and will see through such a catastrophic system as this would become."

Secretary Kirkpatrick senses I am done with my rant and says, " You are blessed with more common sense than any 100 people I know. Your ability to find the reality of the situation and the effects and possible repercussions never ceases to amaze me. It is an honor to work in your administration. I will put something together, and get back to you with a plan to end this Obama abomination."

"Oh – I like that!" I say, "That's a good one!"

I said goodbye and showed them the door. Jerry checked on me but I told him to take a break and be back at 1730 hours. I closed the door and called Cindy.

"Hello, sweetheart," she answered. "Oh, how I miss you."

"Honey, I didn't know how busy a person could be, but I do now," I said, "and I need you in the worst way."

"I want to come there to see you," she said, "and I'm not taking no for an answer. It's going to be Christmas in a couple of weeks. I want to see my husband."

"Okay," I concurred. "When school is out for Christmas, bring Natalie and leave Drew with your parents so he can play ball. You will stay at the White House with me. I can't wait."

"I love you, Adam," she whispered, "and you are my best friend. I really miss you."

"You'll be here soon, and I'll prove to you how much I love you," I said with a little chuckle as we hung up.

I needed to get ready for the 1800 hour nationwide address. Jerry showed up at 1730 hours and I finished my thoughts about the address

He went ahead to the makeup people and told them I'd be there in five minutes. Getting makeup to be in front of the camera wasn't a new experience, but I was never comfortable with it. I took my seat in front of a large mirror, with several bright lights above. It was like watching HDTV and noticing the little things you haven't noticed on people before. I could see a few wrinkles I didn't know I had. My makeup artist was a beautiful young lady from Nashville named Ginny Martin. She had worked on some of the country music stars there. At 29 yrs. old, she wasn't a confirmed conservative or liberal. She didn't know what to think of me and I didn't want to bother her while she worked her magic. She always wore perfume that smelled great, and every hair was in place. She took pride in her appearance and her job. Today's job was to make me look good in front of the camera. As soon as she started, General St. Claire walked in and asked, "Are you prepared?"

"Yes," I answered. "It won't take long, but this should calm everyone down."

I walked back to the oval office and sat at my desk in front of the camera. No one was there to ask questions like in an interview. It was all on me. Let's do it.

"5, 4, 3, 2, . . . You're on," said the director.

"My fellow Americans," I began, "Thank you for tuning in tonight and for your patience while adhering to martial law. I hope you have continued to go about your normal lives. I'm speaking to you tonight to assure you that if you are a law-abiding citizen, you shouldn't even notice there has been a change in Washington, D.C. Daily life will not be affected by martial law, except for the presence of troops. But their orders are to keep the peace, not start trouble by harassing solid citizens. They are on your side. But the criminal element in our society is in real danger. Know this: If you are on the wrong side of the law, you will be met with deadly force, if needed. There are big changes coming within the next 60 days. These changes are being phased in as I speak to you tonight. I expect some backlash, but no demonstrations will be tolerated under martial law." I paused for a moment and continued, "I will now announce to the country for the first time the new policy for illegal immigrants living in our country. If you are considered a Dreamer by our government, you must report to the nearest immigration office or ICE Agent to receive a new green card. This will allow you and your immediate family to stay in our country and you will be given a path to citizenship. If you do not report to ICE, you will be considered an illegal immigrant destined for deportation. For all other illegal immigrants, you will have 30 days to gather your belongings and exit our country. Failure to do so will qualify you as a fugitive to be captured and forcibly removed. If you resist, you will be met with deadly force. Those who leave quietly may apply at any port of entry for readmission. Any paperwork you can produce, providing you have been employed and you have no arrests while in our country, will help you in being granted a new green card for legal reentry." I paused again to let everyone digest some of this new information. Now I changed the subject, "Everyone on food stamps or unemployment insurance, or living in government housing knows by now that they must pass drug tests to receive benefits. I expect a million people or so will lose their free ride they've been on for years. If anyone is worried that they can't find a job, notice I just sent about a million illegals back home. I'm sure there are going to be some job openings. My advice to you is to take one of those and support yourself and your family. One of the best places to look for work will be in the sanctuary states and cities. There will be no such thing as long as I'm in charge of this nation's safety. Any governor or mayor breaking this martial law will be arrested and locked up without bail. I warn you, do *not* task me on this. I do not bluff."

My face was stern and I'm sure the camera was close enough to show how serious I considered this topic to be. I'm sure the nation is shocked and the illegals are cursing me. But this had to be done. I closed by saying, "This nation has been accommodating for way too long. I know we are a nation of immigrants, but we are also a nation of laws. We have to decide to enforce our laws, change the laws that don't work any more, and keep our citizens safe. Thank you for your time and remember: Do unto others as you would have them do unto you. May God bless America. Good night."

I leaned back in my chair and watch as the cameras are removed from the oval office. I thought I had gotten the point across to the citizens of this great country. More than that, the non-citizens surely got the message: Pack up your things and get out, unless you qualify as a Dreamer. Things were about to get serious.

Chapter 12

"MERRY CHRISTMAS" IS BACK

There were certain traditions around Christmas time at the White House. The decorating of the tree and the rest of the rooms was the job of the First Lady. She was in charge of coming up with the style and amount of decorating for all the grounds on the White House property. Maybe the citizens have noticed that there is no First Lady here at the White House. Of course, we don't have a President either, but we needed to follow tradition. I decided to bring Cindy and Natalie to the Capitol ASAP. I called Cindy and told her to pack and prepare to live in the White House until after the new year. Drew had to stay in school for basketball. He was averaging 18 points a game as a sophomore for the high school team. If I brought him to Washington, DC, the coach would probably try to assassinate me. We couldn't have that. Drew knew how much I loved watching him play. I coached him through Junior Pro and AAU basketball for many years. He learned the right way to play—unselfish, hard-nosed, determined, and clean. His mechanics on his jumper were pure. His ball handling was excellent. His decision-making was second-to-none. He was a player with a future at the Division One college level. He wanted to be here with his family, but he was loyal to his coach and teammates. I loved him and missed him. Any father would be proud to have him as a son. I was no exception.

Cindy and Natalie arrived the next day and both were awestruck as they walked into the White House. As soon as Natalie saw me, she ran and jumped in my arms.

"I missed you, Dad," she proclaimed.

"And I've missed you, too," I replied. "Have you grown an inch or two?"

"Maybe," she answers, "but do you know what I want for Christmas?"

"Well, that didn't take long," I replied. "Your mother and I will talk about what Santa is bringing you this year."

"Natalie, it's my turn to hug your father," Cindy said kiddingly. Natalie lets Cindy move into my arms and we hug for what seemed like a longer amount of time than we had ever hugged before. We leaned on each other quite a bit during our 18 years of marriage. We had always shown a united front to our children. I would put our child-rearing skills up against any parents in the country.

"Cindy, let me show you to your room, and Natalie to hers, and then I'll introduce you to the people who help me the most on a day to day basis," I said.

I put Cindy in my bedroom and Natalie in her own room. However, Natalie wouldn't leave her mother's side just yet. She joined us as Cindy unpacked. I explained to Cindy what I expected of her concerning the Christmas decorations.

"You may think you're some kind of big shot here in the Capitol, but now I'm here," Cindy sternly proclaims. She didn't last two seconds until she burst into laughter along with Natalie and me.

"Evidently you don't know who's in charge around here," I said, still laughing.

Cindy knew what she had to do. The White House staff would help her and Natalie continue the tradition of the decorating and lighting of the Christmas tree. We walked down to the oval office and I opened the door and stepped inside.

"You just walk into the oval office whenever you feel like it?" Cindy asked.

"You look surprised," I answered, "but you do realize this is my office now?"

Natalie was super impressed and she was looking at me like I was some kind of superhero.

"Dad, you are the man!"

Of course, General St. Claire was standing in the doorway just as she blurted it out.

"Yes he is, my dear," proclaimed the General. "General Scott St. Claire at your service."

Natalie's eyes were wide open, staring at all the medals on his uniform.

"Are you one of my dad's soldiers?" asked Natalie.

"Why, yes I am," he laughingly replied.

"Now I'm embarrassed, General; she doesn't realize." I said as the General cut me short.

"Commander, she speaks the truth, and I can handle the truth," he said in his best Jack Nicholson voice. We all laughed as I introduced Cindy to the General.

"Oh my," said the General. "Your wife is far more beautiful than you described her."

Cindy gave me a dirty look, turned to the General and said, "Most people say I just settled for Adam." The General was having a good time and played right along with Cindy. But he finally relented and gave me credit for saying that Cindy was extremely beautiful.

"Commander Marsh told me only one girl struck him as being more beautiful than Cindy ... and that was Natalie," said the General. Natalie blushed and Cindy nodded in agreement as she hugged her daughter.

"As much as I would like to continue this bashing I'm taking, I need to get some work done," I said. "If I wanted to take abuse, I would go talk to the press."

I had the General introduce Cindy to one of the secretaries to start the decorating process and I went to my desk. The General sat down across from me.

"General, I need to know something of our capabilities in communicating,"

"What do you mean?"

"Do all of our military men have transmitters and receivers on their person, wherever they are deployed?"

"Yes," he answered. "It's standard issue in modern warfare for the most part, but most definitely for special ops."

I questioned, "so, for example, I could be in a situation room and have the ability to hear what is happening and to give direct orders to those men or women?"

"Yes. The satellite link allows you to do that."

"That's going to come in handy in a couple of months."

"What do you have on your mind, Commander?"

"How long have you got?" I asked, laughing.

"Never mind," he said. "I need to go take care of some things—Christmas presents for my wife, and yes, that was plural. It takes more than one for me to get on her good side." I laughed as he left.

Jerry walked in.

"Where have you been all day?" I asked.

"Sir, you were busy with your family and then the General, so I just ran a few errands."

"Were you picking out my Christmas present?" I asked. I couldn't hold it very long; I had to laugh. Jerry looked very serious when I said it. I thought he might have really been doing that. "I'm just kidding, Jerry. You do way too much for me already. I don't want you worrying about a gift for me," I proclaimed. I needed to get some work done, so I sent Jerry to get the Secretary of the Treasury.

About 15 minutes later Secretary of the Treasury, James Winters, walked in. He had the look of a CPA, a serious gaze through his wire-rimmed glasses.

"Hello, Commander Marsh. I hear you need to see me."

"Yes," I answered. "Thanks for coming. I would like to know how much I can spend on my wife's Christmas gift. I'm writing a check out of the *big* checking account." I loved the look on his face as he gave in and played along.

"I'll have to see what the Federal Reserve interest rate is today," he said. "Of course, you realize we're broke?"

So I told him, "Look, my wife's present is at least as important as, say, a new tank for our military. Just put it in the new budget."

Now we were both laughing, but we got down to business. "Secretary Winters, what is the pulse of the financial markets these days? I'm sure they are apprehensive, but are things progressing the way you think they should?"

"The nervousness in the market is real, but what the big hedge fund guys are hearing, pleases them for the most part. They don't think you will raise taxes and if you balance the budget somehow, they feel the Federal Reserve chairman will not raise interest rates. This will help the stock market along with housing starts, company expansions and retail sales."

"Good," I said. "The Wall Street crowd is on board."

Sec. Winters replied, "For now, yes. But you know that can change in an instant. President Trump worked on the tax policy before you arrived, and Wall Street feels you are accomplishing some great things, but too much change too quickly could upset the apple cart."

"I understand," I replied. "Just tell them to trust me and all will be fine."

"I will, Commander Marsh, and I wish you the best of luck and Merry Christmas," he said. I wished him the same for him and his family as he left the oval office.

I worked alone for a couple of hours making plans for my next goal. It was not time to reveal it to the military just yet. I needed more time to evaluate the changes made so far. I had to get some feedback and some numbers to go on before making my next move. So, I found Cindy and Natalie and took them to the White House dining room.

"I'm taking you to a great place to eat for supper."

"Great," Cindy said. "Where are we going?"

"You're already here," I laughed. "I have my own chef right here. Out of the White House kitchen steps my chef, Marco Koperini. He is a big fellow who looks more like my bodyguard than my chef. He sees that I have guests, and waits for me to introduce them.

"Chef Marco," I said, "this is my wife Cindy and my daughter Natalie."

"It is a pleasure to meet you Mrs. Marsh and Natalie."

"Are you too busy to fix us some supper?" I asked.

"Not at all," answers Marco, "I was just reading about the baseball winter meetings hoping my Nationals would make some personnel changes."

"So you're a big Washington Nationals baseball fan?" I asked.

"Yes," answers Marco, " I go to every game I can."

"That's great," I say, "I'm an American League guy and root for the Detroit Tigers. Maybe they will play each other someday, and we can go watch a game together. But right now, these gals are hungry and we need to get them fed."

I turn to Cindy and say, "You can order anything you like. I'm having lasagna, a salad and Italian cream cake for dessert. You and Natalie can have supper and you don't even have to clean up the mess afterwards."

"How nice of you, dear," Cindy said in her most sarcastic tone.

Natalie laughed at me and teased her mother.

"I'll have the same thing as my husband," answered Cindy.

"How about you, Natalie?" I asked.

Of course I get the typical teenage answer. "A cheeseburger and french-fries, please," came from Natalie.

"I'll get right on that," said Marco.

We had a nice supper together for the first time in what seemed like forever. After a couple of TV shows, Natalie was tired and Cindy put her to bed in the White House guest room right across from our bedroom. Cindy and I follow soon after.

We crawled into bed and I asked, "Sweetheart, do you remember the scene in the Game of Thrones, set on the night before Tyrian Lanister is to go into battle for the first time? He tells Shae something in the scene that—"

"I know what you're talking about; and yes, I will," she answered with a wry smile. It had been a great day and it was a great night.

Chapter 13

THINGS ARE HEATING UP

About two months into the takeover, things were really heating up. The procrastinators and non-believers were in for a rude awakening. I was expecting this to happen and I wanted to share some of the reports I received. I had the military personnel on the streets secretly film some of the interactions in government offices around the country. A transcript from one of those occurrences read
. . .

Unemployment Office

An overweight man stepped up to a window and passed a slip of paper to the female clerk behind the glass. The clerk studies the paper, then passes it back to the man.

Clerk: Sorry, sir; your benefits have been discontinued.

The man's eyebrows almost crawl atop his head.

Man: Come again? I got three more months.

But the clerk shook her head.

Clerk: I'm afraid not. You recently cashed your final check. So, your long-term unemployment benefits have been discontinued as of this point.

Man: That can't be so! I've been collecting those for *years*!

Now it's the clerk who lets her eyebrows rise.

Clerk: Excuse me, sir? Years?!

Man: No, no, no. I mean—well, um—do you have any other kinds of benefits?

Clerk: I'm afraid I don't understand what you mean.

Man: I need to survive. How am I gonna survive?

Clerk: Maybe get a job?

Man: A job? A *job*? Where have *you* been? *Nobody* has a job these days! You don't understand.

The clerk just gave him a look.

Clerk: I'm pretty sure I do. Next.

A young man stepped up to the glass and slid a slip of paper to the mustached male clerk. The clerk studied the paper, then looked at the young man.

Clerk: Form's not complete.

The clerk slid it back toward the man.

Man: What—you—mean?

Clerk: What I mean is there's a section not marked.

They stared at each other for a moment. The young man's face just said, "Huh?"

Clerk: (impatient; "duh") Look here at the drug test section. That must be filled out. You have to do that in Room 6 before you come to me.

Man: Oh, I know; never passed one of those things.

Now it was the clerk's turn to lean in close.

Clerk: Then you can't get one of *these* things.

The clerk tore up the slip of paper. The young man stood there, shaking

Clerk: Next!

Outside the Capital Building:

A group of minimum wage advocates marched outside the capitol building, holding signs in support of their cause. Suddenly, a single chirp was heard from a police siren, as a police car pulled up to the protestors and two cops stepped out.

Cop 1: You can't assemble here.

Protestor 1: Why not? We're being peaceful!

The cop shook his head.

Cop 1: This was covered by Commander Marsh on day one under martial law. The right to peaceful assembly has been suspended until martial law is lifted. Come on. Either you leave or we take you.

Protestor 1: Are you kidding me?

Cop 1: (sternly) Sir, I do not have time to argue with you. There's a change a'comin' in this nation. Don't resist it.

Gulping, the protestor lowered his sign.

Protestor 1: (looking around) Come on, guys. Time to go home.

Those were a few examples of what was happening all over the nation. I thought I was getting the point across—we meant business! The number of those receiving food stamps, government housing, welfare checks, and unemployment checks had been cut drastically. People were scrambling for work for the first time in years. The mandatory drug tests were working, and we were discovering that what I feared was true about where the money was going was right on. The drug dealers' customer base was shrinking. Nixon declared a war on drugs in 1971. He didn't know how to fight it, but I do.

I sat behind my desk, speaking with Drew on the phone, "Oh, really? You did that? A- in Algebra? You really are some fine student. You make your daddy proud." In walked General St. Claire, out of breath.

"I'll call you back, kiddo; keep up the good work."

I hung up and turned toward the General. "Everything okay?"

The General needed to collect himself before sitting down. Even after he did, his breathing was still heavy.

"Hey! You're making me nervous."

General St. Claire spoke, "Sorry, sir; it's just . . . your policies."

"I know, General. A little more extreme than we expected, right?"

"No. It's not that. What I came into say is: This is working!"

Then I kind of shook my head and said, "I don't follow—how exactly have you come to that conclusion after only a couple of months?"

"We've conducted our first public research poll. I've got to admit, I was against it at first, but the boys convinced me that getting an approval rating on you was a good way to let the public know we're on their side."

"Okay. Good idea. Wish I had known, but – what if the numbers are bad?"

"Oh, you'll be happy." The General gave a great big smile. "Fifty-six percent."

"Fifty . . . wait, what?!"

St. Claire nodded and said, "I thought it was inaccurate, so I had another group do an independent study. Their number was 56.5, and their averages are quite reliable."

"My goodness!" I was incredulous.

General St. Claire looked at me in agreement and responded, "I know."

I stood up, walked along the wall behind my desk, turned and spouted, "You realize what this means, don't you, General?"

The General, smiling, gave a playful shrug and asked, "Now we can pursue more aggressive policies?"

"That, too. No question. But what I'm thinking is . . ." I stopped walking and locked eyes with the General. I continued, "The approval rating isn't an approval of me. Or us. It just means that the people have always wanted these things. It proves that most people in this country are sick and tired of freeloaders living off the tax money they are paying to the government. The resentment has always been there. The political correctness police deemed it inhumane to not take care of the poor. I agree, if they are unable to work because of a physical disability, or if they run into some bad luck, I don't mind to give them a leg up for a while. But 'a while' became 'forever,' even when they could have gone back to work and taken care of themselves and their families. This is wonderful."

The General left and I found Jerry and told him to get me the Secretary of Homeland Security. In walked Leslie Bullock, our Secretary of Homeland Security. She had been fighting a losing battle for a long time.

Our southern border had been experiencing a full-fledged invasion for years, but it had gotten much worse in the last year. She was in high heels and a nice blue dress today, but I've seen her at the border in her boots and jeans gathering information to bring back to our do-nothing Congress. Well, I've fired Congress, and things can change more swiftly with martial law. I greeted her and asked her to take a seat.

"What can I do for you, Commander Marsh?"

"I would like to know if your people are keeping up with the numbers of illegals we are seeing exiting the country?"

"Yes, we are," she claimed, "and it has been quite an exodus, to the extent we can count them. Only the hard-nosed gang members seem to be staying behind, but they are scared."

"I have heard the same thing, but I wanted to hear it from you," I said, "and I appreciate the men and women in your department and the job they do. You run a tight ship."

"Thank you, Commander; that means a lot coming from you," she said. "I know the safety of our citizens is of the utmost importance to you." She produced a report from her briefcase. It was from a raid conducted on illegals hiding from law enforcement. I looked over it:

Two sheriff's deputies, guns in hand, walked toward the front door of a rural home at night.

Deputy 1: Is this the right address?

Deputy 2: it better be. Checked it three times.

They stepped up onto the porch.

Deputy 1: You like these assignments, Ray?

Deputy 2: (shrugs) The job's the job. We administer the law.

They knocked on the door and wait. No one answered.

Deputy 1: Mr. Gonzales! It's the Sheriff's Department . . .

A barely [audible] sound was heard. They knocked again.

Deputy 1: Mr. Gonzales, you had federal orders to deport yourself and your family 24 hours ago.

A bullet shredded the front door. The two deputies spread out to either side. Two more bullets broke the door open.

Deputy 1: (screaming into his radio) Station, we're gonna need back up at our stop on Apple Barrel Road.

Deputy 2: (jumping through the door) To hell with waitin' for back up, buddy. These guys weren't waiting.

Deputy 1: (running inside) Ray!

A gang of illegals was in the front room of the house. Gunfire erupts. Five illegals were killed and one deputy was slightly bruised from taking a bullet in his vest.

The sun was down when backup arrived. The house was crawling with cops, paramedics, reporters, and some neighbors. A female reporter addressed a camera.

Reporter: People around the neighborhood have complained about this local gang for the past 18 months. I'm here now with one of the deputies on the scene, Deputy Ray Manuel, who's rightfully being labeled as a "hero."

Deputy Manuel stepped forward.

Reporter: Deputy Manuel, you personally took down three of the armed men today.

Manuel nods.

Reporter: Any statement you'd care to make about the incident?

Manuel: (bleary eyed) Seems to me the government had made its position clear: If you didn't get out yesterday, we were coming for you. And, well . . . (shrugs) . . . we came.

"Secretary Bullock," I said, "I want to pin medals on these two deputies. Bring them to me when you get a chance."

She agreed and I ended the meeting. Jerry returned for new orders. I sent him to ask General St. Claire, to tell me who is in charge of our prison operation. Jerry returned and informed me that Colonel Jared Stollings was at the Pentagon and could be there in an hour.

I said, "Let's go eat while I have a chance."

An hour later Colonel Stollings sat in front of me and I asked, "How are we coming along?"

"Commander," the Colonel started, "we identified the clientele you were targeting in about 100 prisons and began transporting them to secure medical facilities. It was easy at first, but the inmates were spreading wild stories inside the prison, making it harder to take them away peacefully."

"Here's the answer," I said. "Have the warden pick the least violent inmate that we could release, one close to finishing his or her sentence and release the inmate back into the prison population. Turn him loose the next day. All of them will think they have hope of a like result. They will return to an orderly exit."

The colonel said, "I consider the percentage of completion at 70."

"That's great," I answered. "The organs are in good shape, I presume?"

Colonel Stollings concurred, "Yes. Most of the time."

"How about the wardens?" I asked. "Are they causing any problem?"

He indicated that almost all the wardens were on board. He assured me there would be no problems going forward. I told him to continue to take care of this and to look into any individual cases involving non-violent crimes that received too harsh a sentence.

"Bring them to me for evaluation; some of them may be candidates for release. This will cover our tracks," I said.

This was a tricky operation. I hoped the wardens were taking extra precautions and keeping them in their cells most of the time. Any riots would bring instant death to all inmates. Colonel Stollings told me there were at least two prisons cleaned out

"Have you started moving in addicts and homeless yet?" I asked.

"Yes, we have," he answered, "and it's working perfectly. The guards love it and believe in what we are doing." The colonel left the oval office.

General St. Claire showed up and asked, "Did you get a good report from Colonel Stollings?"

"Yes," I answered, "but I'm uneasy with the situation. The inmates are asking questions. They may riot at any time. The wardens need to keep them in their cells as much as possible. We're going to release a couple of non-violent prisoners close to reaching parole. This will spread through the prison and calm things down. We will try to speed up the process to a successful conclusion."

"I have to admit, Commander, you think of everything; that is a great idea; I will make it so," he said.

"I would like to go to the southern border, General; is that possible? I want to see the land on which we are building this wall." I added.

"You getting stir crazy here in the White House?"

"Maybe a little, but I'm needing to head that way anyway."

"Uh-oh," he said; "That sounds like another operation beginning to hatch."

"Let's meet tonight at 1900," I said, "Get everyone together."

The General agreed and left to set the meeting.

The 1900 hour meeting came sooner than I expected. I got sidetracked by a couple of phone calls from government officials thanking me for reducing the number of deadbeats they were dealing with on a daily basis. I do love to hear good news, but I needed to have my notes prepared for this most important presentation. This was the crown jewel of my plan. And I was about to reveal it.

I walked into the conference room to some polite applause. General St. Claire smiled and I figured he had told the group about the 56% approval rating. I acknowledged them and took my seat. "Thank you for all the applause, but do you realize that 44% of the people despise me? I said. They laughed, but would they be laughing in a few minutes? "I called this meeting to talk about our next operation. In 1971, President Nixon announced his war on drugs. We have been losing this war since that day. I intend to win it in less than a week. We will invade Mexico and take out the drug cartels. We will divide any money confiscated with the Mexican government. This money should pay for our wall."

"Wait a minute," General St. Claire said with a furled brow. "Taking care of business here at home is one thing, but invading another country is another."

"Let me finish before you criticize," I said. I let the idea sink in for a moment. "Here is the plan: One, I will travel to the southern border to be seen checking out the landscape. The TV stations will cover my every move. When I leave, I will fly to Mexico City for a pre-arranged meeting with the President of Mexico. I will need complete secrecy and security. We will land late at night and meet at a secure location that will be pre-approved by some of our people. Two, at the meeting I will explain to the President what we intend to do. He will be warned not to tip the cartels that we are coming. This will benefit his people and ours. Half the money we confiscate will go to his administration. There will be no negotiation. If he does not cooperate, all foreign aid to his country will come to a halt. If our countries are to remain friendly, the flow of drugs northward must stop. If he fights me on this we may make Mexico the 51st state. I will not give in. This will happen."

The room was full of whispers and small groups talking to each other. General St. Claire was hesitant to speak. I looked at him and asked, "Can we do this?" in a sarcastic tone.

He answered, "Of course we can, but the logistics are a nightmare. There will be collateral damage. You need to rethink this idea."

The General and I had been on the same page for the most part, until now. But he just challenged my authority, and I didn't like it. I turned to him with a clenched jaw, and gave him one of those serious glares I used to give referees who made bad calls in the basketball games I used to coach.

" I don't have to rethink a damn thing, and you need to figure out the best way to accomplish my plan," I vehemently stated.

The room fell silent as all eyes focused on the General as he contemplated his response. He was starting to breathe faster and the glare from his eyes was a menacing one. "Maybe you don't remember who put you in this position," says General St Claire.

"Maybe YOU don't realize that my position allows me to replace anyone who doesn't follow my orders," I answer.

You couldn't cut the tension in the room with a machete.

General St Claire stood up facing me and proclaims, " You can fire me anytime you want, that's true, or even better, I'll just hand you my resignation. I don't like this idea of invading Mexico."

All eyes were on me.

"Calm down, General, I don't want to fire you or accept your resignation. I want you to understand the plausible deniability in this plan," I profess.

"Ok, talk me into this crazy scheme," said an irritated General St Claire.

I begin, "In the US we have legal agreements between states that allow law officers to pursue criminals across state lines. We are going to garrison troops along our southern border and pursue drug smugglers back across that border to their base of operation and destroy it. That's the way we sell it to the public, and they will buy it. The President in Mexico will make a public statement to that effect. The entire operation will seem warranted and the drug smuggling problem solved."

The General spoke up, "None of what you just said answers the question of collateral damage. The deaths of innocents will come back to haunt you. A mission like this one is at high risk for collateral damage."

"Not if we do it right," I said. "I have some ideas I want to run by you." I told the group to get preliminary plans together and meet in the war room in the pentagon in two days at 0400. I knew they thought that was early, but there would be no distractions or interruptions.

"And don't any of you think the General and myself can't have some disagreement at times, and not accomplish our goals. There may be a day I actually see things his way, and I will change my mind," I wryly said while cracking a little smile. The General had to smile and probably realized I was determined to see this through. He had cooled off now, and everyone left the room except for us.

"I'm not used to that, Commander Marsh, and I apologize for my disrespect," he said.

"Think nothing of it General, but I need to apologize to you. I would never fire you, or for that matter, EVER accept your resignation. You got me into this and we are finishing this together. You just have to trust me on this one. I know human nature, and I think the Mexican President will want the same thing we want; an end to the drug trade between our countries. Any collateral damage is regrettable and will be avoided to the best of our ability. But remember, public opinion is important to politicians, not me. I'm not running for office. I want to complete my vision for this country, and turn everything back over to the people. Help me do this."

Chapter 14

THE MEXICO PLAN

I n preparation for my called meeting at the Pentagon, I brought in our ambassador to Mexico, Herbert F. James. He was a temperamental man, and one would think that would not be good for the type of job held. But he got along with President Ortiz of Mexico. I needed to ask him about the President's interests and family. I needed to know how to break the ice with him when we met. Ambassador James couldn't know I was travelling to see President Ortiz, so I just made it seem like I wanted the information to help in trade negotiations. He told me he loved golf and soccer. Well, one out of two ain't bad. I can talk about golf all day, but soccer isn't in my vocabulary. I thought I'd take him a couple of dozen Titleist Pro V1x balls and hope for the best.

Later that same day I received another report from Colonel Stollings. He had communicated with the wardens about my concerns and apprehensions over the possibility of prison riots during our operation. All of them have made the appropriate changes to make sure this does not take place.

"They wanted to thank you for thinking this through, personally, and not just delegating it to someone and forgetting all about it," the Colonel reports. This makes me feel good about this operation and it's one less thing to distract me from my next operation in Mexico. Colonel Stollings left a disc with me with TV interviews from people related to donor recipients or rehab participants. I found a computer and played the disc. I saw this:

Various people on various American street corners, were talking into reporters' microphones (OS) about the new state of the union. One reporter asked an elderly lady, "What do you think of Adam Marsh?"

She answered, "Oh, I think he's just wonderful! Without the new organ program, I would have had a rotten kidney inside of me."

Another reporter from a different network asked the same question. A little boy answered, "My daddy has a new heart because of Adam Marsh!"

Another reporter inquired about an addict entering one of the prisons.

A middle-aged woman spoke, "My brother was addicted to heroin. But now that Adam Marsh has started building a wall on the southern border, he can't find any heroin anywhere. The wall, plus the addition of troops to protect the contractors, has slowed down the illegal border crossings and the drug flow."

The reporter asked, "Has he considered going into a shelter to kick the habit?"

The woman answered, "Oh, well, fortunately, he has plenty of family, and we're taking good care of him at home. But we do think it's so wonderful those prison shelters are available to those in need."

Asked about Adam Marsh, a middle-aged man replied, "I don't care for the man."

The reporter continues to push, "You mean you don't care for him or you don't care for his policies?"

The man retorts. "Policies? Ha! What policies? You call starving families a policy?"

The reporter continued to push, "With the new organ donation and shelter programs, we've seen life expectancies increase drastically, and the homeless population drop to a historical low. How do you feel about that?"

The man sternly says, "Get that thing out of my face."

I don't think he likes me! People like him would never like me. I was not in a popularity contest, but I was glad 56% of the people liked my policies. I went back to the oval office and I ran into General St. Claire.

I told him where I had been and he wanted to see the disc, so I retraced my steps. He watched my disc as I was standing next to him. He handed me another disc to watch later. We watched the middle aged man from the previous scene on television.

I spoke up. "There's a lot of that out there, General."

General St. Claire, responded, "No idea in human history has ever been unanimously approved of, sir. Unless you count things like eating, drinking, and sleeping—and I even know folks who have trouble with those."

I looked at the General and said, "Well, you can put me into the 'sleeping' category. This job ain't for kids."

The General patted my shoulder and then said, "Your approval ratings are strong as steel, sir. Precisely as I expected before we approached you, if I say so myself."

I smiled a bit. I asked, "Did you expect me to have so little fun?"

The General smiled widely and replied, "You're taking on a massive burden. It'll reshape your soul, that's for sure." He leaned in as he continued "For the better, no doubt about it."

The General exited. I turned back to the computer screen to look at the disc the General had given me. On it was an attractive Latino woman. A reporter asked if she was a citizen.

The Latino woman answered, "I studied hard to get my citizenship. I understand people wanting to cross the border illegally, but Commander Marsh has done a good thing, in my opinion."

I nodded.

The reporter asked, "Do you have any friends or relatives that had to leave?"

The woman replied, "Plenty, yeah. Plenty of both. But most of them didn't complain. They have plans to come back. They're going to study and try again."

The reporter and I spoke at the same time, "I hope they do."

I made it back to the oval office and finished my notes for the 0400 meeting. If I could pull this off, I would be able to see the light at the end of the tunnel.

The night was short leading up to 0400, but I was wide-awake as I entered the black SUV to ride over to the Pentagon war room. Security walked me in and closed the door behind me. Everyone was there, and General St. Claire stood at a high-tech table, the surface of which was graced with half a dozen glowing green digital maps. The General was surrounded by a diverse assortment of leading military personnel. And beside him was Mr. Black, a man in a (fittingly) black suit.

General St. Claire started, "Gentlemen, for the sake of initiating operation cartel strike with maximum efficiency and success, I'd like to introduce Mr. Black.

Mr. Black stepped toward the map tables. He said, "Gentlemen."

One lieutenant spoke up, "Your real name, I take it?" The others laugh, but not the General.

General St. Claire continued, "Mr. Black is with the CIA. He's here to share information his branch has spent years collecting. Let's take him seriously." So the men stop smiling. Mr. Black minded the maps.

Mr. Black began, "What's interesting about the major cartels, we've come to learn, is that all their strongholds are located along Mexico's northern border..."

The men eyed the maps as Mr. Black pointed to them with a silver pen.

Mr. Black continued, "They're just like any other major industry in that regard: They remain close to the supply line. In this case, that means getting their products into our states. So if we strike here—and here—and here, we can cripple the drug supply for many years to come. And hopefully the Mexican authorities will never let these cartels rise again."

"I love the way you think, Mr. Black, but I feel like I'm in a scene from Reservoir Dogs," I said laughing. Everyone gets the joke and laughter fills the room. Even General St. Claire had to chuckle a little. I continued, "I trust everyone in this room with my life and the personnel you choose to carry out this mission must be extremely discreet. There can be no leaks prior to launch. The reason surprise is so important relates to the amount of drugs and money we expect to find if they don't have time to move them. I will be traveling to Mexico City in a few days to essentially ask permission from President Ortiz to put this operation into motion. I usually ask forgiveness instead of permission on most scenarios, but I don't want a response from the Mexican authorities when we launch. Hopefully, President Ortiz will get a call that night and he will give the order to stand down. If all goes well with our meeting, I want to launch in 10 days. Go ahead and start staging some equipment along the points on the border. Everyone will think it has something to do with construction of the wall. We will not go in to take prisoners, but lock down any who surrender. We need information on the whereabouts of their tunnels underneath our border walls or fencing. I hope when we arrive, they will send the women and children out. They will be given that chance, but in the end I want the place leveled. I'm leaving for the border to talk with the contractors building the wall and on to Mexico City. I leave it to you General St. Claire."

Security took me back to the White House to pack my things. The meeting went well and we were on our way to solving one of our country's biggest problems. Jerry met me at the door to the Oval Office and asked what was going on. I told him, "If I told you, I'd have to kill you."

He looked at me, wide-eyed and responded, "Never mind," and then laughed.

Then I told him, "I'm going to the border; you hold down the fort while I'm gone. I'll name you vice-commander for a few days."

He looked at me real serious-like and asked, "Really? Me?" I just shook my head and said, "Uh... no." I got him again; he's so gullible.

Chapter 15

ON THE BORDER

The ride to the airfield took longer than usual. Even with an escort, traffic was terrible and I was impatient. I wanted to get this trip behind me and it was taking too long to even get started. I was going in Air Force One. It was all a little overwhelming. I didn't have to wait long to take off. We were given top priority. Rank has its privileges! A couple of hours later, I was standing in El Paso, TX. I was taken to a secure location to meet with five contractors involved with building the wall. I stepped into the room already filled with security and the contractors. As expected, the floor was muddy from recent rains, and the boot tracks from the troops and contractors. The portable tables and folding chairs reminded me of my teaching days in the lunchroom.

I took my seat at the head of one of the long tables.

"Hello, gentlemen," I announced. "I'm Adam Marsh, a housing contractor, turned author, turned Commander-in-Chief. If you work hard you can achieve great things in this country, so there's still hope for you guys. One of you could become President someday and you can brag that you built the wall, or at least part of it."

All five contractors laughed but one spoke up and said, "That might be true, but I wouldn't have your job; it's much too hard!"

Another one spoke up, "It might be a hard job, but you are magnificent at it!"

I thanked them and got down to business. Each one of them had been given GPS coordinates to build between. They were to use identical wall panels, anchor them, and connect to the two contractors building toward them, or one in the case of the end. I was looking for a report and the possible problems they were experiencing or could face in the future. One of the contractors spoke up, "The biggest problem is transportation. The terrain makes it tough to get the panels on time. The manufacturers of the panels are working around the clock to keep up with us."

"I hope I can help with that," I said. "Here is the phone number of Major Jim Stone. He will arrange transport of panels by cargo plane to the nearest airport. From there, cargo helicopters will deliver the panels where you need them. This will speed things up. Unless Major Stone runs out of gas, or in this case fuel, you will be able to pick up the pace. Have any of you spoken to the other contractors? You know there are 45 more doing the same thing you're doing."

A couple of them said they had heard from some of the others that their problems were much the same. Another contractor spoke up, "The design you picked is working great. The water runs right through the slats and the wall doesn't require any drain tile. The top of the wall is round and has the clips to attach razor wire. You would have to be a fool to try and scale it."

"That was the whole purpose," I responded.

The meeting was a success, and I left after I told them to get back to work and thanked them for their attention to detail. I got back in the black SUV and headed to a meeting with the troops stationed on the border to protect my contractors and assist our border guards. After that, we flew to Brownsville and I was taken to the border to meet with the military. It was a mixture of National Guard and regulars. Recently they were rushed by a caravan attempting to climb over the wall and were forced to use tear gas to push them back. I was about to change our response!

Wearing jeans, a plaid shirt, and cowboy boots, I marched before a group of soldiers, all of whom were standing in a straight line. I stopped marching, faced the guards head on, and spoke, "Put some signs on the other side of the border saying 'Violators will be shot if they try to cross.' If they rush you again or throw rocks, you are hereby permitted to fire lethal shots at any illegal male adult person whom you spot crossing the border."

The men froze, then stirred a little, and then traded astonished looks. After a long moment, one guard spoke up, "But, um, sir? If I may . . ."

I said, "Sure. Go ahead."

"Sir," he said, "what do I do with the body?"

"Leave it for the Mexican authorities. I will tell the Mexican President what is going to happen. He will inform his people to put signs up along the roads and pass the word by mouth: no more illegal crossings. He will be responsible for putting it on the TV for everyone to hear. This should have been done years ago. We have gone soft and been taken advantage of for too long. After the word gets out, border crossing will be reduced drastically."

Guard 2 asked, "Speaking of word getting out, what about the press?"

"What about them? They'll report on it, I'm sure. That's what I want them to do. That will help get the point across.

Guard 2 responds, "Well, um . . . What will you say then?

"They were warned and chose to call my bluff. I don't bluff." I stepped up to the guard, and put a friendly hand on his shoulder and said, "Just concentrate on avoiding women and children."

I walked back to the SUV and boarded Air Force One. That would be my hotel for a little while. I flew that night to Mexico City to meet President Ortiz. Things were heating up. I laid down when I got back on board and told the security guard to wake me when we were about to depart. I had to change into nicer clothes to meet the President. We arrived at 2300 hours local time and I was taken to a secure location pre-arranged by my people. President Ortiz wasn't waiting for me. I hoped he would show up soon; I wanted to leave ASAP. About 10 minutes later, President Ortiz and his entourage came into the room. Out on the balcony I stood looking over Mexico City. The Mexican President stepped outside to join me.

President Ortiz reaches out and said, "Cigar?"

"No, thank you."

President Ortiz lit up one for himself.

"I'm pleased you accepted my visit."

"Of course. I'm pleased you offered to make it."

Together we looked over the vast city.

I spoke, "In light of the policy changes I'm making up north, it's important to me that relations between our two nations are not strained."

President Ortiz argued, "Quite the contrary; I admire your bold approach."

"Well, thank you. But just the same."

I turned to face the President. The Mexican President followed my lead. We locked eyes.

I say, "I'm sending the illegal immigrants home, sir. I'm sure you've noticed this by now. You're going to have a lot of upset people pouring back over your borders for about a month or two more. Some of them are not your countrymen. Some will come back in legally. Others will try to slip in again. That could become a problem!"

The Mexican President gently squints his eyes, taking in the news.

I continue, "Illegals coming back across will be shot. I know that sounds harsh, but one example will probably stop it. The caravans coming up from Central America will stop, when the TV coverage shows a dead body from an attempt to cross the border. But the good part is, I'd like to make it up to you, as best I can."

President Ortiz collects himself and responds, "I don't understand. You can do with them as you wish. They were never legally your problem to begin with."

"I appreciate you saying that, and I agree. But I don't like to clean up one mess only to create another. So as an offering of peace, I'd like you to know that my team will be eliminating your drug cartels within the next 10 days. For right now, this is just between you and me."

The Mexican President's face nearly melts off his skull; he's overcome with shock. "Eliminating? I don't understand."

"It'll be done in secret. In the middle of night. Same way we got Osama bin Laden. Only this time it'll be widespread. We're declaring a war, of sorts. But they won't fight back against the US; they're not strong enough. We will confiscate all the drugs and drug money. One half of the money will go to your government and the US will keep the other half. The drugs will be destroyed. There will be some collateral damage, but we will try to allow the women and children safe passage out of the compounds before all hell breaks loose. There will be few prisoners. Only those we can extract information from about the tunnels, etc., will live through this mini-war.

I think President Ortiz came to the realization that the U.S. could own Mexico if we wanted. But I had made this easy for him. It would look like the pursuit of smugglers he knew nothing about. And when the calls came in from his police, he could just tell them to stand down. If I were the Mexican authorities, and the U.S. was doing me a favor by cleaning out the cartels, wouldn't the Mexican police or troops be more than happy to follow a stand down order from their President?

I said, "You're a wise man and a great leader. Beloved by your people. But with all due respect, I'm not asking to come; I'm telling you we're coming. This mess gets cleaned up now."

The Mexican President sighed and replied, "If you insist, then . . . I shall not make a mockery of you."

I answered, "I'm happy to hear that. Nor I of you. This will help both our nations. Oh, yes, I almost forgot. I brought you a small gift." I went over to one of my security men and he handed me a small bag. Inside are some golf balls. I handed them to President Ortiz.

He opened the bag and commented, "Wow, you went all out . . . Titleist."

"That should get me a round of golf with you on our next meeting," I said. "I'll make the announcement about the illegals when I get home. And fair warning: Those who try to return illegally will be struck down. So, I need you to warn your citizens not to ever try to cross the border again."

Understanding shone from the Mexican President's eyes.

I continued, "Then I'll tell my men about the cartels."

The Mexican President lit up the cigar again and said, "You have my full cooperation, Commander Marsh. And I'll see to it that the cartels will receive no advanced warning. You will be doing the Mexican people a most generous service."

We shook hands and I left for the airport. I needed sleep and I was starving. I took care of both on Air Force One as we flew back to DC. The General waited to hear about my meeting with President Ortiz. Operation Cartel was going to happen, but this way, with the President's approval, we would meet little resistance. I hoped the details of the strike were completed sooner rather than later. I worried about leaks warning the cartels the longer it took for us to launch.

One week later in the oval office, General St. Claire came in looking concerned about something. "Commander Marsh, one of our border guards has fired on an MS13 gang member trying to cross the border, and the boy is dead," said General St. Claire.

"General," I said, "You knew this would eventually happen. How do we know he was a gang member?"

The General answered, "The tattoos on his face and neck gave him away. He was carrying drugs and brandishing a weapon. The guard had no choice but to fire his weapon with intent to kill."

"They were warned and chose to challenge our resolve," I stated, "and it didn't turn out like he expected. We will no longer be pushed around by illegals and this will echo throughout the entire world when the press picks up on this."

"Don't worry," replied the General. "They are on the way now to the border. The pictures and report will hit the airwaves very soon."

The press soon had their story and sent it out worldwide. The backlash was expected to be horrible toward me, and it did not disappoint. But little does anyone know, I would have shot that gang member myself if he had tried to cross the border on my watch. And I wouldn't lose one minute of sleep over it. I couldn't wait to see how effective this message would be in reducing the illegal border crossings. I didn't think they would be brave enough to try crossing for a while, and maybe forever. If the U.S. government had taken this stance years ago the border could have been a piece of string instead of a wall. And thousands of U.S. citizens killed by illegal aliens would be alive today. My job was to protect American lives and this is the best way to do just that! However, I wanted legal immigration to pick up the pace. We needed good, honest, hard working people to apply to come to our country and help it grow. What we didn't need was a criminal element or terrorists to get a foothold in our nation. Also, we couldn't be a welfare state and just ignore our border, letting everyone in.

The General set up a press conference for 1400 hours to allow me to put out the fire ablaze in the press. I'd be there.

When 1400 hours rolled around, the pressroom was filled to the max, all the reporters waiting to crucify me. I stepped to the podium and said, "Okay. I'm going to start by letting Brent Wooldridge from CNN ask me a question. I think I know what it will be, and I want to answer it pointblank."

Wooldridge was shocked, almost speechless, but I couldn't be that lucky. He gathered himself and said, "Thank you, Commander Marsh. This comes as a very unexpected, yet nice, surprise. So, here is my question: Why would you give your troops an order to use lethal force to stop poor immigrants from coming to our country?"

I couldn't help myself. Maybe it was just all getting to me or maybe I couldn't stand the ignorance of the liberals, but with a wry smile, I looked right at Wooldridge and said, "Why wouldn't I?"

The whole room tried to boo me out of the room. It didn't work. I raised my hands and finally got them to calm down. I started, "First of all, the illegal that was killed wasn't a poor immigrant wanting to come to America to search for a job and a better life. You know that to be true. He was an MS13 gang member with a backpack full of drugs and he was brandishing a pistol. Once again, I ask you why wouldn't I want deadly force used on such a person in that scenario? I have never treated the press like the former President. I have never called you an enemy of the people, but you must start reporting the news truthfully. News is not supposed to be for entertainment purposes, produced merely for ratings. It has to be informative and correct, not invented to suit a certain narrative. News is not your opinion or mine. It is what it is. No more, no less. This gang member had been warned and he knew what to expect. He called my bluff, but I don't bluff. He paid the ultimate price. Do you wonder about what might have happened to one of our citizens from the drugs he was delivering? So, now I turn to you, Mr. Wooldridge. Answer my question."

"I'm not sure what you want me to say," answered the reporter, "but I would never take another man's life."

"That's why you are a reporter and not a soldier," I replied.

"Yes, and as a reporter I will call this what it is: You are an accessory to murder," explained Wooldridge.

I shook my head in disgust and turned back to the reporter and told him, "You just don't get it and probably never will. You are doing a great disservice to your viewers. Well, here is some meat for you and the rest of the reporters here: I am and always will be an Old Testament kind of guy. I believe in an eye for an eye and making the punishment fit the crime. Our court system has been a joke for years. States without the death penalty have cost taxpayers billions of dollars taking care of horrible criminals sentenced to life in prison. Common sense has been in short supply in our nation for the last 75 years. Deadlines, promises, red lines, and deals have been missed, broken, crossed, and changed by gutless, spineless, lying politicians. All that is over! I am here to regain the respect that our nation deserves in this world, and I will accomplish my mission with or without the help of guys like you. Are there any more questions at this time?"

Hands went up everywhere in the room. I chose Sally Rayburn from MSNBC.

"Commander Marsh, the families of the inmates in our maximum security prisons have not been able to get in touch with their relatives," she stated and continued, "Where are they being kept?" She went on, " and the second part of my question concerns the spike in the number of available organs for transplant. Is there a connection between these two things, or is this a mere coincidence?"

I responded, "It looks like you have put 2 and 2 together and come up with 4. As I told everyone a few minutes ago, I am an Old Testament kind of guy. The relatives of these inmates will not see them again. They have been executed and their organs harvested. Their deaths have meant life to thousands of people needing organ transplants. I don't care that their relatives didn't get to say good-bye to them. The lives of their victims were taken suddenly and there were no goodbyes for them either. While I am in charge, punishments for the worst crimes will be the maximum…. Death! The US Taxpayer cannot afford to pay billions of dollars every year to provide meals, shelter, health and dental needs, utilities, clothing, etc. to people who will never integrate into society again. Their crimes deserved the death penalty, and I sentenced them. The organ donation is the only good thing any of these inmates would ever be able to offer to society. Bleeding heart liberals, who don't have the stomach for the tough decisions, need to leave these decisions to stronger leaders. That's where I come in. I made this decision and I stand by it. Now the prisons are taking in the homeless and serving as drug rehabilitation facilities. I feel this is a much better use of our former maximum security prisons."

The looks on the faces of the reporters were a mixture of astonishment, surprise, hysteria and amazement. They didn't know what to say or ask next.

Finally, a hand raised belonging to Georgia Bender from CBS News. She looked at me with a sad expression and said, "Commander Marsh, you have played God with the lives of these inmates. You have become judge, jury and executioner. I consider you a madman, equal to Adolph Hitler. How do you answer these charges I levy against you?"

I shook my head,. "You are entitled to your opinion just like everyone else. I am not the judge or jury for any of these inmates. They went through our judicial process and were found guilty. I corrected the mistake made in the sentencing. As far as me playing God, the tough decisions I have made make it appear that way. I know I will answer to God in the end, and not to any one of you. And I thank God every day that it is me that is in charge of the repair of our government, instead of you, Ms. Bender, or any of your pathetic liberal allies. Are there anymore questions?"

Crickets! I continued, "I thought not."

I walked out of the pressroom thoroughly disgusted but ever more determined to fix my nation that I love so much. The General followed me to the oval office and patted me on the back.

"Damn!" he said, "You turned the tables on those reporters like I have never seen before. I wanted to stand and salute you."

"That's over for now, but I did vent a little frustration in there."

"They needed that, in my opinion," stated the General.

"Let's change the subject," I said. "When will operation cartel take place?"

"Tomorrow night."

"Good," I said. "I'm going with you."

For the next 20 minutes, General St. Claire told me at least 10 reasons why I couldn't go. I just listened, politely nodding my head in agreement with everything he said: It's too dangerous, what about your family, we need you here, you'll just get in the way. After he finished talking, I interjected, "You know I'm going, right?" He shook his head and laughed. He was fighting a losing battle . . . and he never lost.

I met the General at the military air base. I was dressed for battle. I bought a pair of combat boots and borrowed a flak jacket from the marines. I flaunted my 9mm Smith&Wesson and the General saw it. He laughed and said, "You're really serious about this, aren't you?"

"Sure," I said. "I want to be ready for any emergencies."

"Let's hope you don't need that thing," he said pointing to my pistol.

"I won't if you've done your job," I replied. That got me a dirty look but then a little chuckle.

"Watch and learn," he ordered. "We're leaving now. Come on."

As we flew to the border he went over the plan. We would surround the compounds of the four cartels, giving them no escape. Surgical teams of Navy seals and U.S. Army special ops would slip in under cover of darkness. Using silencers on their weapons, the guards will be taken out and women and children will be evacuated. All hostiles would be eliminated while searching for all drugs and money on the grounds. Any vehicles trying to escape would meet rocket fire from the attack helicopters.

We landed at the Air Force base and transported to the staging area. I stretched my legs as helicopters crossed the sky.

Two young Marines sat inside one chopper. Marine 1 asked, "There's going to be collateral damage, you think?"

Marine 2 answers, "Isn't there always at times like these?"

"Yeah, but these people have families in these homes. Women and children, man." Marine 1 drew his breath.

"From what I've heard, we're taking measures to deal with that," said Marine 2.

Marine 1 said, "Oh yeah? What you've heard, huh? Well, last I heard we weren't doing squat."

I didn't say anything. Soon we were in the air. The surgical teams were on the ground. The helicopters dropped troops in to surround the compounds. My heart was racing. That was a rush like I had never felt before, but I tried to look calm. I had on a headset, so I could communicate with our base camp and let them know what was happening. However, the men all have body cameras and were sending video back to the base. I think they just gave me a "nothing" job to keep me satisfied. I was okay with that.

General St. Claire sat in the chopper wearing a radio headset. He spoke into it, "Now listen up here, fellas: We're using a ton of force. We want this done in less than an hour. That means we must be precise. So, we go in surgically. Just as soon as I get word that the women and children are clear, we finish the job."

On the ground we were getting reports of shots fired, people running, and some women and children being escorted out. All of a sudden we saw an SUV go speeding up the driveway of the compound. General St. Claire merely ordered one of the other helicopters, "Take him out."

That SUV never had a chance. The pilot fired two missiles at the vehicle and made it disappear in a huge explosion. Another SUV tried to make it out the back way. It met the same fate. Reports come in that the compound was clear and we closed in. Troops searched the main house and found a room full of pallets of cash. They were chatting on the radio about the amount being unbelievable.

The troops started to move the cash in bags to their helicopters. Other men were entering the drug lab adjacent to the main house. The guards gave up and were questioned about any tunnels. Neither one would answer. Captain Keith Goldston's team of Navy

Seals was in charge of the situation. I switched to their channel on my headset. Captain Goldston told them he would let them live if they could tell us about the tunnels. One of them started to speak up and the other slapped him and went after the captain. Bad idea! He was killed in front of the other guy.

"I guess he didn't want you to tell us," proclaimed Captain Goldston, "I'll ask you one more time, and if you can't take me to the tunnel, you will meet the same fate."

We found the tunnel. Everything went off without a hitch. This was the military at its finest. We had the money, located the drugs, and found the tunnel in 20 minutes. Ten minutes later we were loaded up and backing out of Mexican soil.

That was when I heard the General say, "Paint the target and proceed." Somewhere near the compound and lab was a soldier with a laser. To "paint the target" meant he was telling the air force jets somewhere above, that their laser guided missiles had a target to take out. The missiles just appeared out of the night sky from high above. The explosion was beyond my imagination. The compound was completely destroyed. There was nothing, and I mean nothing, left of the compound. It was a good thing all those compounds were areas to themselves with no structures of homes close by. The whole operation was a huge success.

"I never even had to draw my pistol," I told the General

He just laughed at me as we got back to camp.

The other teams arrived back at camp bragging on the success each of them experienced. Each team was comparing the amount of cash each one of them found at their perspective compounds. As the bags of cash were loaded on to our plane, I couldn't help but think about President Ortiz. He kept his promise and allowed us to catch the cartels off guard. I didn't know the amount of his reward yet, but I was sure it would be magnificent. I intended to call him as soon as I got back to the White House.

The flight back was a long one and I got little sleep. I ordered the cash taken to the Pentagon and locked in a safe room to be guarded around the clock. I was taken to the White House, arriving at 0300 hours, just in time to get a quick shower and fall into bed. But who could sleep with the images that were rolling around in my head? The fighting, the SUV blowing up, and the missiles leveling the compound at my location; those things kept coming to the forefront of my consciousness. I dozed off eventually, but morning came too quickly.

I sat behind my desk, my facial muscles tense. I looked as though I hadn't been sleeping. It was late morning, and I got a visit from General St. Claire. I stood to greet him in the oval office.

General St. Claire said, "You don't stand for me, sir. I stand for you."

I responded, "I stand for all that's good and right."

Smiling we shook hands. At the same moment, we both sat.

I asked, "What's the good word?"

He replied, "Well, all told, we took out all four locations including their labs. There was nothing left. If the Mexican government is smart, they will never let the Cartels re-form."

I said, "I'm calling President Ortiz after you leave. I just wanted to hear the official word from you and what the press is saying."

"Before I leave, I have something else."

"Well, tell me some more good news."

The General slapped a folder on the desk between us. "Here are this morning's estimates of the drug trafficking into the United States as of right now. Following last night's operation, I expect these numbers to drop significantly."

I snapped up the folder and started flipping through it. I paused, looked up, and said, "I don't understand how we could have let the drug flow get this bad.

General St. Claire declared, "What's not to understand, sir?"

"I can believe it," I said. "It says, um . . . drug trafficking is at an all time high. It has to drop drastically."

The General had a glow in his eye. He asks, "Was that not the intention of last nights operation?"

Nearly speechless, I answered, "Yes, and it happened so easily."

"Success never happens easily, sir. It was quick for us . . . but it took you to make it happen."

I nodded.

Nodding back he says, "Sir," and left.

I walked to the door of the oval office to find Jerry. He was waiting at his desk. I sent him to get the Secretary of the Treasury. A few minutes later Secretary Winters walked in. I told him I wanted a count of the cash confiscated in the raid, presently under guard at the Pentagon. I told him I needed a total ASAP.

"I'm on it, Commander."

I picked up the phone and called President Ortiz.

His assistant called him to the phone, and he answered, "Hello, Commander. It's good to hear from you."

I answered, "I'm sure you don't know this, but I was there last night to witness this historic event. I wanted to be able to give you the true story. I don't want there to ever be any lies told between us."

President Ortiz agreed, "Those are my sentiments exactly. Do you consider the operation to be a success?"

"Yes, I do, Mr. President," I answered, "but I want to hear from you. Are there any problems I don't know about? We were in and out in less than an hour and it was dark. The massive explosion leveling the compound was enormous. I hope there was no collateral damage, and I need to hear your answer on that subject. We tried very hard to avoid causing any."

"Commander, as far as we know at this time, the only casualties were those of Cartel members," said President Ortiz. "Your raid was so late at night, all the lab workers were gone. They are the locals forced to work for the cartel for slave wages. I consider your operation a complete success. The people around the town in close proximity to the compound felt the blast from your missiles, but no one was harmed. Their mood this morning, I'm told, is one of amazement and extreme happiness."

"I am so happy to hear you say that, Mr. President," I said smiling, "and I want to let you know that we are counting the cash we confiscated as we speak. Sir, it was quite a haul. It is a mountain of bills of all denominations. I am looking forward to getting a final number and wiring your government the half I promised you. I want to thank you again and remind you that you owe me a round of golf in your country someday."

President Ortiz laughed and promised, "I will most definitely deliver on that. Thank you, Commander."

We hung up and I was relieved to find out there were no other causalities other than our intended targets. For the first time since the 1971 war on drugs began, we were winning.

A few days later, the General called a meeting of the military leaders at my request. The White House conference room was filled with the very same leaders of the Cartel strike operation.

I sat at the head of the table, laying praise on my leading military personnel, "Gentlemen, we all know the media's busy analyzing the results of our recent actions, but I'd like to just take a moment here and touch upon the actions themselves. Never before in our military's history have strikes been carried out with such speed, precision, and conscientious humanitarianism. You men, and the men and women who served you, have proven flexible amidst rapid innovations, effective amidst changing conditions, and brave amidst dangerous circumstances. I'll be, um . . ."

That was strange. I seemed to be at a loss for words, and that was never the case. I tried to speak, "I, um . . ." I couldn't help but shed a tear. I continued, "I'm forever in your debt, men." I sniffed, wiped my tear away, stood and said, "Don't tell anybody about what just happened."

The men all laughed.

One lieutenant spoke up, "Sir?"

I turned to face him.

"Do we know about the cash yet?"

"Yes, we do, Lieutenant," I answered, "but what is it you would like to know?"

He laughed a little and admitted, "Some of us have a little pool to guess the amount we seized."

Of course, I'd already heard about this pool, so I was procrastinating. "Before I tell you, I did hear that one of your men was accused of taking some of the money during the raid," I said.

The lieutenant started to smile because he knew to what I was referring. General St. Claire had Captain Goldston plant a wad of $100 bills in one of his men's backpacks. The General called for a spot inspection and discovered the cash in front of his whole team. Everyone was in on the joke except the one poor soul. He started to deny taking any money and was about to explode, when they all broke up laughing at him. It was hilarious and the poor guy took it well. General St. Claire told him, "Son, since you took it so well, I'm going to let you keep half the money." Then the rest of the team had a funny look on their faces. The soldier looked at the General and asked, "Really?"

"Uh…. no," said General St. Claire.

I was never going to mess with General St. Claire; he was tricky.

"Oh, yes, Lieutenant. You were wanting to know the total of the cash collected," I remembered. Everyone was really curious, so I finally spat it out, "It was $21,462,131,410. Half goes to Mexico and the other half will help build the wall."

Another one of the military brass spoke up, "Commander Marsh, I would like to speak for everyone in this room and say we are extremely proud to be under your command. We have never had such a determined leader to do what needs to be done to solve the problems of this nation. I dare say there will never be another like you. We all really appreciate what you have done for the country. But we are worried: even though your numbers are high, the country seems contented. But, um . . ."

General St. Claire interjected, "You are taking a beating in the press, sir."

I absorbed these words, gave a nod and said, "I've been meaning to have a word with them. General?"

General St. Claire confirmed, nodding, "We'll make it so."

"Thank you, again, men," I said. With a wink, I walked away. Meeting over.

Chapter 16

DEALING WITH NEGATIVES

Another press conference was scheduled for the next day. Maybe it wouldn't be as contentious as the last one.

I stepped up to the podium. The press corps was all eyes and ears. Also on hand were military and White House personnel.

I began, "I'll take questions when I'm through with my remarks. We live in radical times, don't we? Times of massive change. Breakthroughs in our way of seeing things. Drastic new actions on the part of our government. I've been pleased to hear words of approval regarding this administration's conduct. Though meanwhile, of course, the press has a proud and historically anchored duty to engage in inquiry.

This was, of course, to be expected. You will inquire upon the pages of your publications, and you will inquire here, face-to-face with me. So in anticipation of your thoughtful and moral inquiries, please just allow me to say the following . . ."

I took a deep breath and continued, "Nothing I have ordered—not a single thing for which I have wielded our military's talent and might—has had any negative impact whatsoever on the people whom I like to call ordinary Americans. Ordinary Americans constitute a rather large group. They're you and me. They're most of the folks watching this at home. They're the people who fill our proud communities, large and small. They're the ones who keep their heads down, do their jobs, take care of their families, and make a real difference. They make the world a brighter place. They exist in a positive spirit, one of health, heart, and stability. Now, I know ordinary Americans well because I am one. Though perhaps in recent days I've shifted to the "extraordinary column . . ."

Everybody laughed.

"But at heart, I remain a most ordinary and humble soul. Which is why I would not mess around with my ordinary American friends and neighbors. Accordingly, please allow me to make this perfectly clear: Eliminating our maximum-security prisoners has no bad impact on ordinary Americans, for most of us are not heinous criminals. Scaling back our entitlement programs has no bad impact on ordinary

Americans, for most of us are not selfish freeloaders. Sending our illegal immigrants home and building an impenetrable fence to keep them out has no bad impact on ordinary Americans, for ordinary Americans happen to be, American!"

The audience laughed. Some applauded and cheered.

"So as you conduct your wise analysis, bear in mind the impact that I've had on ordinary Americans. In many cases, that impact has been entirely neutral. In many more cases, that impact has opened up staggering gateways toward greater opportunity and abundance. I mean, after all, I've redirected billions of dollars that were going to waste so that money can flow back toward the people! And just wait "till I fix baseball and those 4-hour long games."

The audience laughed again and applauded. I can't help myself; I have some comedian in me.

"I tell ya, that'll be one heck of a job, fit for discussion at a later point in time, but for now, I promise you this much: Corporate tax rates will remain low so the jobs we saw go overseas can continue to come back home, where they belong. And the money that these corporations have been spending overseas can now be put back into our factories, for the sake of creating jobs—not lining the pockets of the folks up top. I'll be very certain of that. Meanwhile, I know more and more questions keep cropping up about foreign policy. And I take them seriously, I do. But my aim from the get-go has always been to get our own house in order before we go out attending to the whole global neighborhood. And rest assured: If you think I was tough on our enemies here, you cannot even imagine what I have planned for the enemies that torment us from afar."

I could tell the mainstream press wasn't buying it. No matter what I said, they weren't going to agree with me. I thought they hated President Trump, but they may hate me more. But like him, I at least had FOX news. They defended me most of the time, but of course they have to be fair and balanced.

I don't waver and continue, "In conclusion, before I take your questions, I know I'm looked at in many circles as a madman. The press paints me as a monster. The leaders of the old political parties paint me as a fanatic. Religious leaders pray for my repentance. But as you go about the business of analyzing me, I want you to remember what I've said here and now—"

Gathering my breath, I said, "I am an ordinary man. I never had any political aspirations. I had artistic aspirations: to write a book. And then, wouldn't you know it? One thing led to another. And here we are. Working to eradicate a system that I long knew was doomed to fail. The old way was self-serving, corrupt, and wasteful. It rewarded those in power and treated the criminals better than the victims. The old way offered a maze of complex regulations, far too obscure for the common man or woman to understand, and reliant upon costly lawyers for interpretation. The old way was a thorny tangle of red tape, slow progress, and checks and balances that threw us *way* out of balance. So, I'm begging you—just for a little while—to keep trying it my way. No red tape. No slow progress. No self-serving, mixed-up waste. 'Cause if you think you've seen some interesting results so far, then you have no idea what's on the way. God bless America." I adjusted my tone, "I'll take your questions."

I thought I had covered everything, but the press . . .

A reporter on the room's left stood and asked, "Commander Marsh, the leaders from both major political parties have issued public statements pledged full willingness to cooperate with you and your administration. And yet they find themselves being ignored. Why not work with these leaders in a spirit of bipartisan compromise?

"Well, my friend, I've had many an opportunity to examine the historical record. And unfortunately, those parties blew the chance they had. That chance lasted for almost 250 years. For a lot of it, things went all right, but in general, compromise simply does not work within our system. If I have the solution to a problem, I sure don't want to water it down by mixing it with someone's bad idea on how to fix the same problem. This is just common sense. This is a concept foreign to liberal minds. Let me ask everyone in this room a question. I want everyone to pay close attention to this. SOME OF YOU IN THE BACK AREN'T

EVEN LISTENING! I feel like I'm teaching a bunch of 8th graders! I don't care who you are, you need to hear this!"

I wanted to get their attention, and I had it now.

"So here's my question: How will we ever know who is right?"

I paused and stared them down.

"How will we ever know who is right?" I repeated.

"The Democrats or the Republicans? The Liberals or the Conservatives?"

I paused.

"You see, in this polarized atmosphere, neither side gets to solve problems 100% the way they choose. So once again, I ask, how will we ever know who is right? At this moment in our nation's history, an ordinary American Citizen is applying common sense to deal with the different array of problems in our country. If my solution doesn't work, I will try yours, but I'm batting a thousand so far. Congress used to compromise and pass a few laws, but right now, Congress and the nation as a whole is so polarized that all we have is gridlock - and a terrifying budget deficit. Sound familiar? Next!"

A reporter on the room's right stood and asked, "What is your reaction to the comparisons between you and Adolf Hitler?"

My expression went stoic and I replied, "Well, for one thing, I'm certainly not the first American leader to earn such a distasteful comparison. Seems all you have to do to drum up that remark is do something somebody somewhere disagrees with!"

Some of the reporters chuckle. I was sure CNN was loving that.

But I never wavered, "But in all seriousness, here's what we have to understand: Hitler had an ill mind. He was a fanatic; he killed innocent people strictly on the basis of his/her religious convictions. Adam Marsh, on the other hand is ready to lay down his life for equality of religion in this country. Do I have a special place for Christianity? Of course! I'm Christian! So are most Americans. We put "In God We Trust" on our currency! And I've no shame in celebrating my Christian faith; yet, I bear no intolerance for any other religion our people choose to practice. It's none of my business. As for those individuals whose lives have not continued under my leadership, we're talking about a supremely violent class of savage criminals - friends to no one. Many of them handed light sentences for no good reason, or caught within our borders after being asked to leave. I eliminated them to bring money back to our decent, ordinary citizens, and to make room for homeless people and drug addicts to start climbing upward again. And the moment you catch me eliminating someone for a reason that does not benefit my friends and neighbors—or majority of decent, ordinary Americans—I invite you all to start calling for my head. Yet until that day, I'm sorry to disappoint you. But I think Adolf Hitler was a monster. Who's next?"

The beautiful Madison Shepherd of Fox News stood, "Do you have a date in mind for when you might turn things back over to the people?"

"Madison, that is the best question any reporter has ever asked me." I answered. "It will be soon, and I'm looking forward to the transition back to my normal life. Thank you for that great question."

More reporters stood, but I waved them off. That question was a good one to end the press conference, so I shut it down. I really wanted to get through to those people, but it might not have been possible. I'd try again later.

Later that night in the Oval Office, I sat in a chair in the corner in my bathrobe, nursing a glass of milk with ice. The moonlight shone through the window. I had a faraway look in my eyes, thinking about the press. A knock landed on the door. I looked up, put my glasses on the windowsill and said, "Come in."

General St. Claire entered the room.

I said, "Jeez, you weren't kidding about that insomnia thing. What time is it?"

"I hadn't heard from you all evening. I didn't stay for the press conference."

"Is something wrong?"

He stopped in the middle of the room and said, "No. I came to ask you that."

"Oh, I'm fine," I said. "The press is aggravating but I can handle them." We both smiled. "Thanks for checking on me, though."

"Of course."

Smirking, I said, "You could've called though, General. Maybe sent a text message?"

With a smile in his eyes the General said, "I don't text."

"Didn't imagine you would."

He pivoted as if to leave, but said, "There is something that would be good to discuss in person."

On edge I said, "Okay . . ."

He pulled up a plush chair, aligned it with mine and started, "Few weeks back in one of our meetings, I questioned your decision to invade a foreign nation and I shouldn't have done that."

I reassured him, "Oh, General. Come on; you don't have to do this."

He responded, "No, no. Stop it. I do. It was the wrong thing to say. And more wrong still to think. I wanted you in this position. We gave you the right. The *system* gives you the right."

We made eye contact.

The General declared, "I was a fool to ever doubt you."

"You weren't a fool. You're a wise man. Always have been. And besides, it's not like you called me Adolf Hitler."

I smiled, but he did not. We parted company and I tried to get some sleep.

The next morning, I called President Ortiz to let him know about the cash total. He was thrilled with the news, yet I sensed there was something bothering him. And then he asked if I was sitting down. That couldn't be good.

"Commander Marsh," he said, "I was a little premature in my assessment of your operation the other night. I indicated to you that no bodies were found, other than Cartel members. This turned out to be wrong. One of the labs had 6 women working a night shift preparing cocaine for shipment. Two of the women had to bring their children with them, since they had no babysitter. The children, three in total, were asleep in an underground, hidden room that your men must have missed. When the shooting started, they went to their children. None of them survived the missile attack that leveled the compound. Our authorities were notified that there were people missing in the adjacent town, and they feared those people were at the compound during the raid. We found the bodies all huddled together in the hidden room."

I was at a loss for words. There was dead silence on the phone.

President Ortiz asked, "Are you still there, Commander Marsh?"

"Yes, sir. I am, but I am too sad to speak," I answered. "This is very disturbing news and I feel responsible."

"It's not your fault, Commander, and your men would not have known where this room was hidden."

"I take it the news media has picked up on this story?"

He assured me it has and there would be some backlash.

I told him I wanted to think about it for a couple of days and I would contact him later. We hung up the phone and I was paralyzed. I sent Jerry to find General St. Claire. I told the General about the conversation between President Ortiz and me.

"I knew it was too good to be true," lamented the General. "It's so very hard not to have collateral damage in an operation like the one we launched."

I know what he said was true, but I was only interested in cleaning up the Cartels, not killing innocents. It was an unfortunate situation and I had to do something for the relatives of the deceased. Nothing would make up for the lives of those women and children, but I was going to try.

I called President Ortiz later that week and told him what I wanted to do for the town and for the families of the deceased. It was no fault of their own that they were working the night of the raid. President Ortiz had told me of the methods of hiring used by the cartels. They threatened the families of the women in nearby towns to force them to work long hours preparing the cocaine and other drugs for delivery. To resist meant sure death to those closest to these women. To protect their children, they must comply.

I sent the government a million dollars to purchase five acres of land where the compound had been. It was to be deeded equally to the families affected.

Another million was sent to prepare the land and build a new road to the property. Six houses would be built for the nearest relative of each person that lost his or her life. I sent 3 million dollars to complete the houses with yards and landscaping. Another 5 million dollars would go to the town for any improvements they needed, but a memorial for the slain must be erected in their honor. I hoped this would be enough and that the people would never forget the misery brought about by the rise of the Cartels.

President Ortiz, thanking me for my generosity, said, "The world needs more men like you to lead. You are tough, but compassionate, and you lead using common sense. We will always be friends. Good luck."

"Thank you, President Ortiz," I said. "You can count on me, always. Good-bye."

I told the General what I had done, and he approved whole-heartedly.

Chapter 17

DISAGREEABLE PEOPLE

July in Washington, DC, is a really hot month. I guess the sun shining on all that concrete makes it more miserable. Of course, the press keeps the heat on me, but I can take it, being from Alabama. Seven months into this takeover, things were starting to settle out. The maximum-security prisons had been cleaned out and the homeless and drug addicts had taken their place in the jails. Thousands of people needing emergency transplant surgeries were saved in the process. The drug addicts living on the streets and the homeless had been rounded up and brought to emptied prisons. The flophouses full of needles and filth were being cleaned up in every city. Prisoners in the local jails were doing the work; the rehab of the addicts in the prisons was done cold turkey. I wanted them to feel the pain of rehab in hopes that they would never want to repeat their mistakes.

The number of food stamp recipients had gone down drastically, as had extended unemployment recipients. The unemployment rate was at 2.9%. After the illegals were forced out of the country, there were job openings everywhere. When the welfare ran out for those who couldn't pass a drug test and they got hungry enough, those jobs were gobbled up. People were starting to understand that you can't afford to pay people not to work or let welfare recipients spend government money for their drug habits. There was more government housing available after the drug tests were required to live there. Many people had to move out due to their drug habit. The neighborhoods were much safer with all the gangs eliminated. But that came with much sorrow. A few of the gangs in the inner cities had members who were forced to join. They were pressured to do evil things by the gang leaders. Many boys would have preferred to leave the gang, but it wasn't safe to do so. Retaliation by those gangs was ruthless and cruel, so those boys were trapped. The military had orders to eliminate those gangs by any means necessary. Most of them were killed in gun battles, but a few surrendered and went back to their families, with a warning to never return to gang activity.

The illegal immigrants were a different story. Many of them tried to stay, when I ordered them out of the country. Many of those illegals came through our southern border, but they weren't from Mexico. They didn't really believe we would enforce this ultimatum. Several of them fled to the sanctuary cities, but that didn't work. It helped to catch them because they were all in one place. I dared mayors to buck me on this, and some thought about trying me. But the ICE agents were allowed to do their jobs backed by the military. Anyone that surrendered was taken to the border port of entry and forced to leave the country. Those who resisted were shot. After just a few deaths of illegals trying to flee, most just raised their hands in surrender. All my domestic policies were working as planned. So why was the press still hounding me? The answer was power. The people the press preferred to run this country were liberals, socialists, and maybe even communists. It was hard to understand when you know that everyone wanted to come here to chase the American dream, yet they wanted to change it to look like the place they came from. To become an American citizen one must learn our language, abide by our laws, respect our flag, and assimilate into our culture. Anyone that can't do that shouldn't be here. The latest approval rating on all my domestic changes was at 60%, which was still not good enough in my eyes. I wanted more of the country to believe in my methods and results.

Summer had allowed me to spend time with my family. We were finally all together for the first time in 7 months. Drew had a great year in basketball and

Natalie was practicing golf every day she could. Cindy and the kids were here for another three weeks and then back to the grind. Cindy reminded me every day of my promise to fix everything in one year. I still thought I could do it. I was trying really hard.

Foreign policy had been taking up a lot of my time. Even though my family was with me, my time was limited. We couldn't really move around much; it just took too much security. So, we stayed in the White House most of the time. The kids would get bored and probably want to go back home early. I was a kid once, and I understood. Their friends became more important than old mom and dad.

Of course the lives of my wife and children changed drastically when I decided to join General St. Claire as the face of the U.S. Government take-over. My major concern in the beginning was the health and safety of my immediate family and in-laws. My children were the most important consideration and Cindy agreed. We knew they could adapt to any changes because of their demeanors and intelligence. They were extremely book smart, but common sense had to be applied in the situations that were bound to come up. Not everyone would be singing my praises and my wife, children, parents, brother and in-laws would need to learn to hold their tongues. There would be security around them 24/7 and any confrontations would meet with a swift and firm response. The less they argued with those around them the less the security personnel would have to step in. It was easy for me to say that, but I wasn't going to be there. I couldn't go home until this thing was over.

Things went smoothly in the early stages of the takeover, but as time went by, my policies started rubbing a few people the wrong way. It wasn't the hard-working average American; it was the freeloader living off the generosity of the U.S. Government and the state governments. When I cut them off from extended unemployment benefits and demanded a drug test be passed before receiving food stamps or welfare checks, I expected there to be trouble eventually.

Cindy informed me on one confrontation she had at our local grocery store. Natalie had accompanied her mother to get groceries, not expecting what happened next. A man in his 50s, overweight, poorly groomed, and irate over losing his benefits, recognized my wife and started berating her over my policies. He was calling me a traitor and a dictator. He even said I was a Nazi. Cindy was in shock and Natalie was standing behind her mother. Security moved in swiftly and escorted the man out of the store and I was told he might have a bruise or two from falling down.

Another incident happened at Cindy's office. One of Dan's clients wasn't on board with the takeover. He was a dyed-in-the-wool democrat and extremely liberal. He hated me more than he hated President Trump, if that's possible. He knew Cindy worked there and stopped at her office one day to complain about me. The two security guards just inside the door made it quite clear that if he didn't remain civil, he would be physically removed from the premises. He proceeded to tell Cindy how wrong I was about what the government needed to do for the citizens.

Cindy politely said, "You are entitled to your opinion, even if it's dead wrong!"

Wow! Now that was my girl. I thought the first confrontation prepared her for this second one and she showed a little fight in my defense. I love my wife!

Natalie wasn't immune from the criticism toward me. Kids could be cruel and at 13 years old, things could get really nasty. One of her classmates expressed her dislike for me, one day at school during lunch. The grocery store scene had prepared her for the next situation she encountered. As her classmate pointed her finger at Natalie and started saying nasty things about me, that I'm sure she heard at home from her parents, security stepped in to end it. Natalie said, "Don't stop her; let her talk. She will just prove how stupid she is!" My kids were competitors and they didn't back down.

Drew had his troubles at school and at basketball games. Having a U.S. history class while his father overthrows the same government he's studying was not an ideal situation. One day in class the discussion got heated between a disgruntled classmate and Drew. The teacher was half-heartedly trying to stay neutral but seemed to take the side of the other boy. His father had lost his benefits and couldn't support his family.

Drew asked him, "Did he pass his drug test?" The boy went silent. They all knew the answer to that question. The teacher told the boy to sit down, but he didn't comply. He started pointing his finger at Drew and walking toward him. Security took him to the principal's office and he was put in a different class going forward.

Basketball games were much harder for security. Drew had to be on the floor competing and that wasn't an ideal situation. More security was required for the gates, dressing rooms, bleachers, and lobbies. Of course, the opposite team's crowd was trying to get under Drew's skin by holding up signs of me in a Nazi uniform. They called him a traitor, like his father. None of this stopped him from leading his team to 24 wins with only three loses. But one night during the game, one of the players on the opposite team purposely elbowed Drew in the head. Security saw the whole thing, but kept their seats. I had warned Drew of things like this during his days of playing middle school games. Well, my warnings finally came true. The security guards told me later that Drew waited until the next quarter, watched for the referee to turn his head away, and elbowed the guilty player in the jaw and almost knocked him out. They didn't even call a foul. That was my boy! I love my family.

Of course my parents had to endure a few heated arguments with some of their liberal friends, but nothing ever escalated to the point security had to step in.

However, my brother Roger wasn't so lucky. During an argument to defend my actions, one of his co-workers at the plant he worked at, took a swing at Roger and connected slightly. Roger has a temper and tackled the guy. He broke the guy's jaw before security could pull them apart. He was lucky he didn't lose his job, but the boss realized Roger had relatives in high places.

My in-laws had a few heated discussions but all in all survived the ordeal unscathed.

The thing that everyone had to get used to was the presence of security 24/7. My children's schools had more security than any school in the nation. And, yes, it was a little intrusive and inconvenient, but oh so necessary. I would never be able to thank all the security personnel enough for all they did to protect the people I loved.

Chapter 18

SUCCESS AND FAILURE

The Secretary of State had been a regular visitor recently. All foreign affairs were on hold for the most part. The General was handling the military end of it, while Secretary Richey, our chief diplomat, handled the negotiations and interactions between nations. Most nations were in a wait-and-see mode when looking at the circumstances in the U.S. at that time. They didn't know what to think of me or how long I would be in charge. The press probably helped me a little without knowing it, when they described me as a mad man with my finger on the nuclear trigger. I knew that I wanted my life back and this had to end. The U.S. was the policeman of the world. We had to get back to doing that job. I was not qualified, nor did I want to tackle it. But tackle it I did.

As I predicted, the family visit was cut short due to boredom. I was happy to see them for a couple of weeks, but I knew that they weren't enjoying it much. It was more for Cindy anyway. She was coming back later when I would take one more run at convincing the liberals in the northeast to stick to my program once I was gone. It would be a hard sell. But the foreign affairs of the nation suddenly took center stage.

In the Middle East, our ally Saudi Arabia is the major player in the Organization of Petroleum Exporting Countries or OPEC. Until recently they were the largest oil producers in the world. But thanks to new discoveries and new technology, the United States has overtaken Saudi Arabia as the number one oil producer worldwide. But the Saudis are huge in the export business of oil throughout the world. As one of the Saudi's large tankers sailed southward along the coast of Somalia, pirates hijacked the ship and all its crew. Secretary Richey kept me abreast of the situation and suggested we let the Saudis handle it themselves. The pirates demanded a $5 million ransom and soon got it. But the negotiation was costly. The pirates killed 6 of the crew to make sure the Saudi government knew they meant business. They reached out to Secretary Richey, asking for help to rid the area of the Somali pirates and make the Gulf of Aden safe for travel by all ships. Secretary Richey advised me to take a wait-and-see stance and monitor the area for tankers passing through the Gulf of Aden. That's not my way. I called

General St. Claire and had him bring Admiral Jason Segers with him. The three of us met the next day and I asked for their opinion on the situation. Admiral Segers filled me in on the capabilities of our nuclear submarines. I liked what I heard.

"General St. Claire, will there be any repercussions if we destroy a few pirate ships?"

"Do you really care?"

"No," I said, I don't. They will be getting what they deserve and anyone who disagrees with that puts themselves at risk, I won't stand for pirates killing our friends."

Admiral Segers responded, "I've been wanting to hear this from one of our Presidents for years. Just turn the U.S. Navy loose, and we will solve this problem for you."

I ordered, "General St. Claire, set up the situation room. I want satellite imagery of the area, monitoring all movements in the Gulf of Aden and southward toward Kenya in the Indian Ocean. Tell me how many submarines you can send to the area, Admiral Segers, armed for the destruction of pirate ships. This will be a warning to all nations that dare to kill our friends. Let me know when the activity picks up in the area and come get me. I want to be there to give the final order to put these murderers in their place—the deep six."

A week later things were in place. Satellites were wonderful for watching terrorists like these pirates. They don't realize they are being watched. The ability to see such clear images of these criminals preparing to hijack another ship is amazing. There were three such vessels, all cruising the coast of Somalia. Our submarines were quietly stalking all three. The crews of these pirate ships were armed and the satellite images were proof enough for me that they were intent on taking another tanker. There was a large tanker flying a Saudi Arabian flag heading right for the pirates about 25 nautical miles away. I wasn't taking any chances that some of the Saudi crew could be killed if we waited too long to destroy the pirate ship. It had no identification, so I felt sure I was doing the right thing.

"Admiral Segers," I ordered, "take them out!"

"Yes, sir, Commander," he answered. "I'll be honored to carry out your orders."

The communication officer sent the submarine the signal to attack. It was over in a couple of minutes. The pirate ship took two direct hits from torpedoes launched while submerged. They never knew what hit them. The submarine surfaced to assess the damage and found some debris floating along with the bodies of several pirates. The tanker arrived shortly and was informed of what had taken place. The crew of the tanker cheered as they floated past our vessel.

The other two ships met the same fate. The message was loud and clear to the pirates of Somalia. Death could come at any time from our submarines. The U.S. Navy was not to be taken lightly. There was a new commander in charge and his name was Adam Marsh.

Martial law couldn't last forever. The troops were getting tired and they needed a break. I told General St. Claire I was going to New York to give a speech in September, and the whole country would be watching. I wanted to convince them we were right to do what we did.

General St. Claire spoke up, "Oh, sir. I don't think you should go."

I responded, "No, no, no --- maybe it's not a bad idea. Foreign policy is on the horizon for next month, but in the meantime, I'm attending to the budget, regulations, immigration, and the wall. If I went to New York and gave a speech on these matters, maybe I can win that part of the country?"

He returned, "Sir, um . . . With all due respect . . . Our system is no longer democratic at this time. It doesn't matter if some people disapprove."

"It matters to me, General. Let's block off a couple of days."

The General agreed but said, "If you go up there, I will be in charge of security. I don't want any screw-ups."

September rolled around before I knew it. Cindy came to ride with me in Air Force One to New York City. The speech I'd prepared would be delivered at a high school football stadium. I wanted to show the people of New York, I was one of them and not have to deliver the speech in an opera house. I was just as comfortable in that setting as they would be. But General St. Claire was not happy. Security was going to be a nightmare. They had been working on security in the area for a month, but I was determined to use this as my venue. It was a short flight and I was taken to the high school where a dressing room was set up for us. Two security personnel escorted Cindy and me to the room. One of them was a woman I'd seen only once before. She was very serious about her job; I had not seen her crack a smile. Her name was Gloria McPherson, thirty-eight years old, of Irish descent, and tough as nails. She was assigned to protect Cindy and me and she wasn't letting us out of her sight.

I sat before a mirror, getting my make-up done by a young female make-up artist. Cindy sat in a chair against the wall; I could see her reflection in the mirror.

Cindy said, "You've got nothing to be nervous about, honey."

I averted my gaze from her and looked at my own reflection. I replied, "Well, that's good news 'cause I'm cool as a cucumber."

With eyebrows up, Cindy said, "Really? Is that why your hands are shaking?"

I looked down at my hands. Indeed they were. I turned to the make-up artist and said, "Could you excuse us for just a second, dear?"

Nodding, the make-up artist gathered her things and left the room.

I turned my chair to face Cindy. I said, "Hey, you shouldn't talk that way in front of the people. She's gonna run and tell all her liberal friends."

Cindy smiled, "She loves you, Adam. She told me before."

We eyed each other, gazing deeply. Cindy continued, "What's the matter? You seem far away."

I shrugged a little and said, "I'm just . . . a practical man. Always have been. I got a creative streak in me, too, but it's practicality that makes me who I am. And that's a good thing—most of the time. But the bad news is . . . its practicality that makes me know this thing can't keep going so smoothly 'til the end of time."

"What do you mean? You mean the system's bound to fail again?"

"It's simple math, I've smashed many of the dependable equations. And numerous good things have occurred. But I can't know what I don't know. And it's those unknowns that might grab me in the end."

Cindy smiled and rose from her seat. She said, "How 'bout just focusing on what you *know* then?" She leaned over and kissed my forehead.

The make-up girl returned and finished her job. It was time to go. Gloria escorts us to the stage. A bright sun shone down upon small town New York. I stepped up to the podium as a large crowd applauds my presence.

"Thank you all! Thank you, New York!"

Little by little the applause died down so they could hear me.

"Now, I'm here to address some important items. To be sure, they're not as colorful as my other agenda items leading up to this point, but as far as I'm concerned, they're more important. I want to talk about the future. I see this takeover ending soon. And how we function as a nation afterward is critical. I want to find out from the common, every day, normal citizens, like me, if we can work together from now on to make our country the best place in the world to live. The division in our nation has hampered our ability to conduct our daily lives with ease and simplicity—and common sense seems to have gone right out the win—"

BLAM! BLAM!

The crowd screamed as the two shots rang out.

I was down behind the podium. The first shot hit me in my left shoulder. Instantly, Gloria, my security to my right, dove across my body. The second bullet hit her in the back right shoulder. Shrieking, Cindy, who was seated just behind me, ran to one side revealing my wound. By that time, 6 security guards surrounded me and saw gushing blood from the wound on Gloria. I'm conscious enough to point to the direction the shots came from. I had felt the bullet move the air across my face from the right to my left.

Cindy yelled, "Oh-no-honey! Oh-no-oh-no-oh-no! Oh, my God!"

The General swept in and put his jacket under my head. Secret service men swarmed around him and I said, "General, get Gloria to the hospital; I'll be fine."

The General barked orders to get Gloria into an ambulance. I tried to sit up, but the pain stopped me. "Can you make it to the van? I don't want to wait for the ambulance."

"I can make it!" I leaned on the secret service men and staggered to the van. The doors flew open. The General stuffed me inside. Cindy climbed in. The General climbed in. Two secret servicemen climbed in and slammed the door shut. Up front another secret serviceman started driving.

Cindy is distraught and uttered, "How did you let this happen, General?"

General St. Claire responded in a kind voice, "We're going to save him. Think positive." One of the secret servicemen took off his jacket and used it to apply pressure to my wound.

Cindy, still frantic, said, "I heard two shots. Did they get him two times?"

General St. Claire answered, "Only one. The other shot hit Ms. McPherson. Sloppy bastard."

Cindy broke down crying and whimpered, "Not sloppy enough."

Then General St. Claire assured her, "He'll be alright. Flesh wound." He whipped his head toward the front. "FASTER!"

I heard the engine gun louder.

Cindy buried her face in her hands and cried, "We should have never done this."

General St. Claire answered, "Don't say that, Cindy."

Cindy argued, "It's true! Nothing is worth this!"

The General thought for a minute. He looked at Cindy and said, "Your husband saved the country." Collecting himself he continued, "And he will not die. Keep it together, Adam!"

My eyes swam in their sockets, but I was still aware of what was happening. The General looked at Cindy, and Cindy looked back. Then I coughed; it was an anguishing sound and it hurt a little. I was bleeding, but I was not coughing up blood.

Cindy's crying intensified. I had to talk to her if I could clear my head. But then in a shocking moment to everyone in the van, I said, "So much for liberals, huh, General?"

Astonished, the General looked at me then laughed.

I laughed, too, as Cindy took my hand and begged, "You can't die, hon. You have to hang on."

I gathered my breath, "I'm not going anywhere. All the liberals have done is pissed me off." I was worried about Gloria, and I asked the General to radio for a report on her status.

"She's going into the ambulance now and she's talking to the EMT," he said.

"You know I'm pinning a medal on her; she took that second bullet for me," I declared.

General St. Claire agreed, "If you don't, I surely will."

Cindy said, "I may buy her a car or even a house for saving Adam."

"Are you sure? I'm . . . are you . . . sure . . .?" I passed out.

Chapter 19

THE RECOVERY

I heard words and asked, "Where the heck am I?"

Cindy appeared above me and kissed me softly on the cheek several times. "You are in the hospital and you're waking from your surgery to remove the bullet," she explained.

I wasn't in intensive care, so I couldn't be too bad off. Sunlight streamed in through the room's window.

General St. Claire appeared at the foot of the bed and said, "We have security everywhere and everyone is okay except for you and Ms. McPherson."

"I want to go see her," I said as I tried to get up.

"You're not going anywhere, Mr. Marsh," said the nurse. "I've got my eye on you."

When I felt the pain in my shoulder, I changed my mind anyway.

The General spoke up, "Do you want me to say it now or wait a while?"

"Go ahead," I said. "Let me have it."

"I TOLD YOU SO! The whole idea was a security nightmare."

"Did they catch the shooter?" I asked.

The General laughed and said, "Well, now that's a long story, but you've probably got time. When you pointed from the direction you thought the bullet came from, the security team was on the hunt. They radioed the helicopters and started to monitor any movement from the distance they felt a shot could have been fired. The helicopters sent word to the mobile units to follow certain suspicious acting vehicles. The hero was your old friend Craig Archer from the FBI, who brought you to us on the first night we met. He approached a pickup truck with a New York plate, and the guy driving tried to run Craig over. The chase was on. The helicopters were following above, and there was no way the guy was going to escape. He made it to a rural farmhouse and crashed through the door of a barn. He got out of his truck and started firing a high-powered rifle at the agents. Craig returned fire from behind his vehicle. Soon there were secret service, FBI agents, military personnel, and even a local sheriff. They called in his plate number and got his name and address. We found out later, he had been cut off from his unemployment benefits and had told some of his neighbors he would kill you if he ever had the chance. Evidently, the neighbors were on his side because they didn't bother to tell anyone. The stand off lasted all of about 30 minutes and that is when New York's Seth Hunter charged out of the barn, firing at all the men surrounding him and was shot to death. His body must have been hit with 40 rounds of ammunition. There will be no trial, no life in prison, and no pleading insanity."

I answered, " Well that's good. Quick and efficient. Don't need to be wasting money on some trial." I winked, and the General laughed.

He looked at Cindy and smiling said, "Seems like he's going to be just fine."

Cindy said, "Yeah. Unless this happens again."

I shook my head and said, "Nah, sweetheart. It's not gonna happen again; I'm out."

General St. Claire looked at me, perplexed and asked, "Sir?"

I declared, "Oh, not right away. I just need four or five more months. That'll be plenty of time. Then this whole system will get some new leaders. Elected ones. New President. With my approval rating at 60% and maybe even higher after this fiasco, the country might just elect someone with common sense, conservative values and a work ethic. I hope both political parties vanish and candidates just run on their ideas with no affiliations. We will need a new Congress. We need to elect people that will work together to find the answers to our problems. At least I will leave them with a lot fewer problems to solve. Surely they won't get back into the same rut we were in before our takeover."

General St. Claire asked, "Four or five months? Isn't that a little . . . rapid?"

"Just the way I like it. Then . . . time to slow down, play golf. Maybe some speaking engagements. Heck, I'd like a chance to enjoy our country now that it's new and improved."

Everyone in the room smiled.

The next day my shoulder was really sore. They gave me some pain medication that morning, shortly before the doctor came in who performed the surgery. He brought a surgical mask in and asked me to sign it.

"Who do I write this to?"

"Doctor Benjamin Morris," he proudly announced. "It's the closest I'll ever be to a President."

"Now, you know I'm just a Commander in Chief, not an elected President."

"I know," he said, "but you have saved this nation from itself. I will never forget what you have done for our country."

"I'm honored to meet you, Dr. Morris, and thank you for everything."

I signed his mask and listened to his orders for the day: No sudden movement, no excitement, just stay calm and rest. He left and a nurse took his place. She was really cute, in her early 30s and blonde.

"Where's my wife," I asked.

"Right here," said Cindy as she entered the room, "and you're old enough to be her father."

I laughed, but that hurt. The nurse blushed and Cindy winked at her to let her know she was just kidding.

"My wife's a comedian sometimes."

"Oh, that's okay, Pops," she chided.

Cindy laughed loudly; I tried not to laugh.

Someone needed to get me some information on Ms. McPherson. How is she doing? What is her status? Those were my concerns that day. I raised my bed up and stepped on to the floor.

"Where do you think you are going?" asked Cindy.

"To see Gloria if you can give me her room number," I said.

"She's in room 3212," Cindy answered.

"I'm walking there now," I said.

I put on my robe and headed down the hall. The secret service agents snapped to attention as they saw me enter the hall. I told them to follow me and to pick me up if I fell. I made it to her room and knocked on the door. She answered, "Come in."

When she saw me she tried to get up but fell back in bed. Her wounds were a little more serious than mine.

"Ms. McPherson," I said, "I can never thank you enough for what you did. You didn't have to do that, you know."

"Oh, yes I did, Commander Marsh. It's my job and I take it seriously."

"How do you feel?"

"A little rough, but I will be fine. How about you?"

"About the same as yourself. I'd like to know how you became a secret service agent."

She began, "My parents were both army officers. They loved this country and instilled their values in me. When I graduated from high school, I joined the army to get my college paid for. I served my time, went to college, and graduated with a degree in criminal justice. I applied with the U.S. Marshall service and was hired as a trainee. Eventually, I got interested in serving the office of the Presidency as a Secret Service Agent. I put in my time, worked my way up, and this is what it got me."

We both laughed at our plight but not too exuberantly. We both hurt when we laughed.

"Gloria. May I call you Gloria?"

"Most certainly,"

"You know my golfing buddies will give me a hard time about having to be saved by a girl," I said.

"I can imagine, Sir," she said with a smile.

"Well, I'm just going to tell them to kiss my—"

"Honey!" Cindy interrupted from the door. "You need to get back in bed."

"Gloria, get some rest and we will be seeing each other in the near future. I will be pinning a medal on you for your bravery."

"Thank you, Sir."

I headed back to my room for some rest. Cindy was by my side. She told me the children were quite scared until she was able to call them and tell them I was fine. I couldn't wait to see them and reassure them that their father wouldn't be denied the goals he set for this country.

The General showed up after lunch, and I told him to get back to the White House. I was going to fully recover and be back there soon. He argued with me because he hated to leave. He felt responsible and wanted to stay. But he finally relented and admitted I was right to send him back. He knew as well as anyone in the country what I wanted done if any problems arose while I was recovering. And besides, I was only a phone call away. He left that afternoon and traveled back to Washington DC, leaving me to recover from this assassination attempt. Air Force One was fueled and ready for my trip back as soon as the doctor released me. That happened two days later and Cindy and I left New York.

I was ushered to my bedroom in the White House where I rested another day. The next day I was in the Oval Office. I called Jerry in and told him to call a cabinet meeting. We convened at 1500 hours. I walked in the conference room to a standing ovation.

"What's that for?" I asked.

The General spoke up, "For being brave enough to go to New York, for surviving a bullet, and for continuing to lead this country."

"Thank you for those kind words," I replied, "but I don't deserve all that. I just thought I could bring some more people over to our way of thinking and I failed."

"Sir, I beg your pardon. You did not fail," said General St. Claire. "Your poll numbers are the highest they've ever been nation-wide and the highest they've ever been in New York."

I was stunned by such good news. I didn't know the assassination attempt had brought about such positive results. I sat down and started the meeting. Each member reported on activities occurring while I was incapacitated. All of them had done an excellent job of keeping the focus on the changes we'd made.

Secretary Kirkpatrick stood up and asked for the floor. I said, "Sure, what do you have for us?"

"Commander Marsh," he begins, "what you have accomplished in such a short period of time is remarkable. Are you sure we need to go back to the way things were before you took over? Maybe our system of government was always doomed for failure. Maybe this dictatorship, for lack of a better word, is what we need going forward. I hate to see all your hard work go down the drain after you leave."

"Stop right there, Secretary Kirkpatrick," I reply, "I appreciate your compliments, and agree with you about our government being doomed for failure. The election of Obama was like hitting the fast forward button on the remote control for government ineptitude. I saw the end coming when our national debt reached $20 trillion. The politicians couldn't buy votes fast enough with all their give-away programs. Common sense went out the window in those eight years and the media saw no wrong with anything that happened during that administration. And yes, we have fixed many of our problems without red tape slowing us down, but the people will want to get back to normal soon. They just want things to work better on the reset. I'm going to start winding this thing down. I hope to be done in four to five months."

There were some sad faces looking back at me, but they knew I meant every word. I wanted my life back if I could get it.

In the next few months, I started to reduce the number of military personnel on the streets a little at a time. I wanted to see if any new gang violence would arise or any other criminal activity. I knew the "out of sight, out of mind" influence would rear its ugly head when the troops disappeared. But the local police, sheriffs and deputies, state troopers, border guards, ICE agents, and law enforcement in general would command a great deal more respect. Criminals would be dealt with much more harshly than before our take-over. Punishments would have to be much tougher from then on.

The wall was 75% done on our southern border. Crossings by illegals were down 85% more than the previous year. I thought it was time. I called a meeting of the military council that originally approached me. It was April, a year and four months into the takeover.

General St. Claire waited for me to take my seat and asked, "Is this the end?" I guess he sensed it was coming. After being shot, I had told him in New York that I was ending the take-over.

"Yes," I answered, "and I want to thank all of you for all the help you've given me. This has been a grand operation. Most people never thought anything like this could ever happen here. But it did, and it has been a tremendous success. I will call a press conference tomorrow and announce the conclusion and ending date of this takeover. I will set dates for new elections and swearing in ceremonies. I will leave General St. Claire in charge of the government and the cabinet. He will run the day-to-day operations at the White House. I would like to leave the White House and go back to my home by the 15th of the month."

General St. Claire stood and saluted; the rest of the officers did the same.

The General spoke up, "Everyone in this room has thanked God every day for sending us Adam Marsh. We all wish you and your family the best. God bless you, Commander Marsh. It has been our pleasure to serve under you!"

I spent a few minutes thanking each man and shaking hands. I told the General to call the press conference for 1400 hours tomorrow. He sadly agreed.

I entered the pressroom the next day at 1400 hours. It was full. Looking fully healthy, I took my usual spot behind the podium. The members of the press, military, and White House staff wore wistful smiles, while some wiped away tears.

I began, "As you know, this will be my final press conference. The last year has been a wake-up call for all of us—myself included, but I'm proud to say that I'll be leaving this government in far better condition than I found it. And I'll watch with eagerness as our new politicians man their posts. And as they do, I hope that they keep their minds on the popularity of what my team and I have accomplished here. The last thing we need is to get under the American people's skin. Oh, yes, they are a patient bunch . . . but I imagine they'll grow less patient if they see any old trends creepin' back around."

Some of the crowd laughed.

"Just so there is zero confusion, allow me to summarize what has been achieved during this grand season: one, the age of the freeloader has reached its end, and more people than ever are showing up to work, helping themselves; two, no more illegal aliens exist within our borders, yet we have, of course, welcomed many of our old friends and neighbors back on legal terms; three, unemployment stands at 2.4%

and that's a number I hope to see come down; four, drugs and drug dealers have all but vanished from our streets and those who still suffer from addiction are receiving excellent care; five, the Mexican drug cartels have been stricken from the face of God's green earth; six, justice has at least greeted the monsters who soaked up billions of our dollars by staying alive—for no good reason—in our maximum security prisons; seven, our streets are now clear of homeless people, and those who once struggled to find stability and shelter are also receiving top assistance; eight, our tax code is simpler than my dear Aunt Mildred's shopping list; nine, our nation's debt headed downward and our budget's creating a surplus; and last but not least, ten, we have welcomed Christianity back into our schools. No longer does the faith of our founding fathers meet with unfounded suppression. Christianity inspired our Constitution and shall, therefore, enjoy the same robust promotion as all our people's other wonderful faiths."

I took a good, long look around.

"Now I must say, looking at this list, if I had to do it all over again, I wouldn't change a thing. Okay, well, maybe except for the whole getting shot part."

Everyone laughed.

I continued, "I encourage ALL the decent Americans who succeed me at this post to lead our nation forward with a firm, sure hand, providing an equal shot at success to all and making sure any and all punishments always, always fit the crime. And please: Put your faith in our people. Give them your trust. If you ask them for more, trust that they shall give it. And by the way, I'm referring to matters of good and evil, not matters of taxation.

The crowd laughed again.

I went on, "Every day, from here on, I shall remain with you all in faith and prayer, praying for the future of this great nation. As you might have noticed, I'm something of an Old Testament kind of fella. And you can rest assured our military and I will be keeping an eye on how the coming months and years unfold. In other words, don't make me come back!"

Everyone howls with laughter and applauds

I finished by saying, "Thank you all for your much-needed indulgence! I love this country. God bless you. God bless this office. And GOD BLESS THE UNITED STATES OF AMERICA!!"

I threw two fists in the air. Camera bulbs flashed. The room went wild, except for the liberal media. They clapped politely, but I felt it was because I was leaving. Amid the crowd behind me, I found Cindy and I nodded at her. She nodded back and smiled. I went to her, took her by the hand, gave the crowd one final wave, and walked away.

No more "I'll take your questions now." No more living in the White House. I'm going home for the first time in nearly a year and a half. It was like the ending of a Hollywood movie. But it was the real world. I had a lot to consider. Would my family be in danger for the rest of their lives? Will I, and my whole family, need security around us at all times? Cindy and I discussed all these possibilities the night before I accepted this challenge. We knew our children would be affected, but I wasn't sure we realized to what extent. Needing security 24/7, even after I finished the job, was quite intrusive to a couple of teenagers. My son's basketball team would always have an extra man or two riding the bus to away games. My daughter's golf matches would include a couple of extra "caddies." Would my wife and I ever be "alone" again? Maybe after elections were held and the new leaders began to conduct the nation's business again, the focus would shift to them instead of me. I could dream.

That night I had the chef prepare a dinner for the White House staff, the secret service, the cabinet members and all spouses. Military personnel took over security for the evening. I was able to thank every person for his or her loyalty and support. Anyone there that night didn't have to remain in his or her job and perform duties for a group overthrowing the U.S. Federal government. I couldn't imagine what was going through their minds at that time. Were they going to be seen as accessories to this treason? Would they lose their jobs eventually? Should they resign and distance themselves from it all? I had a great deal of respect for the people in that room, and I told them so. Evidently, the day I was introduced to the nation and the world as the new Commander-in-Chief, those people liked what I said and decided to give me a chance to prove my point.

I singled out a couple of individuals at the dinner. My assistant Jerry Mathis was invaluable to me the entire stay at the White House. He never failed me in any task I gave him. I noticed the day General St Claire brought him to the Oval Office to meet me; he had an old flip-phone. I chided him about it several times and told him he needed to update his equipment. He argued that the new phones cost too much on his military salary. To show my appreciation, I gave him a new cell phone with a two year paid contract, and an autographed copy of my book. He thanked me as he shyly walked away from the podium.

"Don't thank me yet, Jerry; the number on that phone is number 1 on my speed dial," I joked, "and it's fixed to where you can't block my number." Everyone laughed as Jerry blushed and took his seat.

The chef had been a most important figure during my stay at the White House. He and his staff prepared all my meals. I barely left the White House once we took over the government, so I had to eat my meals there. I couldn't just order a pizza to be delivered to the home of the leader of the free world. I thanked him for the great food and presented him with season tickets for the Washington Nationals baseball team. He didn't know what to say, but he thanked me and gave me a hug.

The next morning, I started packing all my things to take to Air Force One. It would be my last ride on this awesome aircraft. Cindy was helping me and asking me to speed it up.

"You know you went over your time limit?"

"Well, I got shot, you know," I argued. "I wasn't exactly planning on that."

"At least I had your insurance paid up and I could have been a rich widow with many suitors," she chided.

"I was wondering how you felt about my full recovery," I joked.

We both started laughing and I kissed her. Then I kissed her again.

"We don't have time for this," she said.

"Shot down again," I said. We laughed again. I loved my wife more than she would ever know.

Jerry showed up and took care of moving our things to the airfield. I went back to the Oval Office and ran into General St. Claire.

"Adam," he said, "this might last another 250 years or it might need to happen again in a year, but what we have accomplished is extraordinary. This coup was not done to crush the citizens and place the military in power for several years; it was done to fine tune a plan set forth by our founding fathers. It was done to fix a broken system. This takeover was a battle between good and evil. With God's help, good won out."

"I agree whole-heartedly with you, General, and I hope it does last for at least another 2 ½ centuries," I declared, "but we won't be around to fix it next time."

We laughed and saluted each other. Cindy and I headed to the SUV to take us to the airfield. We were going home.

We landed in Birmingham that evening and headed home to northern Alabama. As we approached our hometown, we noticed the lights were on at the high school football field. Suddenly our SUV turned toward the high school, which wasn't the way to our house.

"Hey, driver," I said, "you didn't need to turn there."

Cindy started smiling, and I knew there was something going on here. Sure enough, I'm taken to the high school and we drove right onto the football field where the stands were packed on one side. There was a podium waiting for me to say a few words. The cheering went on for at least 5 minutes with a standing ovation like I had never experienced. My kids and in-laws were on the portable stage, along with my parents. As I gazed at my parents and all the people in the stands, I began to get a little emotional. I had been on edge for 18 months and I was starting to wind down. My emotions were getting the best of me. I wondered if I could even speak.

When the ovation finally stopped, everyone got deathly quiet, waiting for me to say something. I took a deep breath and began, "The last time I was in a foot-ball stadium, things didn't turn out so good!"

The stadium erupted in laughter.

I continued, "I hope I can feel a little safer here at home compared to New York!"

There was more cheering. I felt a little better then.

"I sincerely appreciate the welcome home," I said. "I've really missed being here with my family, but I've been a little busy."

There was laughter and cheering.

"I see you brought my parents here today," I said. "Without their guidance, I would not be the man I am today. I would never have been able to lead such an operation that we launched 18 months ago. And I could never have taken on the responsibility of funda-mentally changing the country, if I had not been raised in northern Alabama."

There was another standing ovation that lasted a couple of minutes. I was shocked at the passion of these friends and neighbors in my hometown. I had no idea they felt that way about what I had done for the nation. They could have been embarrassed that one of their own had participated in this treasonous act, but that couldn't have been farther from the truth.

"I want to thank everyone here today for your support and the faith you had in me," I said. "I want to get back to watching my children compete in sports, excel in school, and grow up to be good citizens of this great country. I want to grow old with my beautiful wife right here in my hometown. Thank you so much. God bless Alabama and the United States of America."

I was exhausted, but I hung around to shake hands and mingle with everyone that wanted to talk a while. It was 2 hours later that the security detail ushered me into my home. Cindy and the kids hugged me and welcomed me back. I get to sleep in my own bed tonight. Tomorrow I would start to lead a normal life again.

What was I thinking? My life would never be normal again.

Made in the USA
Middletown, DE
23 January 2021

32244011R00126